PATRICK

Kevin G. McGuire

I HOPE YOU
ENJOY MY
STORY

PATRICK
Kevin G. McGuire

Published by Kevin G. McGuire at Smashwords.
Copyright 2013 Kevin G. McGuire

To my brother Brian, whose heart was always purer than mine.

Preface

In 1968, at the age of seven, I was struck by an intoxicated driver while playing baseball. This accident left me paralyzed from the waist down and has since forced me to use a wheelchair. Every summer following the accident, I was required to check into a New York City hospital for one week of physical evaluations and tests.

At this hospital, I was treated by the same physical therapists, nurses and doctors; I was also assigned the same room. This room was invariably occupied with individuals who were from different ethnic, social and economic backgrounds. They were admitted to the hospital for various reasons.

I quickly realized that no matter how different my roommates were, the bonding that took place during these short visits was incredible. It was amazing both in celerity, as well as intensity. Our injuries, sicknesses and the hospital room seemed to insulate us from the prejudices and hatred of the outside world.

I also discovered that as quickly as this bonding took hold in the hospital room, it left just as quickly as we returned to our natural environments. All the promises about visiting and keeping in touch vanished as soon as we were discharged. More importantly, the prejudices that dissipated within our hospital boundaries reappeared as we left our cocoon.

At the age of seventeen, I shared the most intense seven days of my life with three roommates at this New York City hospital. I will always love but never see or talk with my roommates again.

I entered the hospital that week not yet an adult, but left no longer a child.

PATRICK is inspired by those seven days.

— *Kevin G. McGuire*

PATRICK

Jack Flannery exited his prized, sacrosanct, black Ford Falcon Station Wagon, purchased with faux wood side paneling as an added accessory, when he heard the ruckus emanating from the cheering crowd. Before heading toward the excitement, Jack noticed a three-inch jagged scratch on the front passenger door just below the handle. Being auto-neurotic, he wondered how this flaw slipped past him. Already his day was now unexpectedly spoiled, but he continued walking across the aged, cracked sidewalk to the edges of the baseball outfield fence. Jack would, however, occasionally look back to see how noticeable the imperfection was from the increasing distance.

The late afternoon end-of-summer sun was slowly descending, casting shadows on the heat-weathered field. A light, comfortable breeze swayed the leaves of nearby mature oak trees.

"Striiikkkke," yelled the masked umpire behind home plate.

Two high school teams were playing in the highly anticipated Sectional Championship Game. He recognized many of the families who packed the designated home concrete stands, dressed in various blue and gold school color attire, behind first base. A smaller, but still fervent group of visiting fans, wore selected red fashions and sat in the rusted bleachers behind third. Both sides chanted for their respective players.

Regardless of the still-sweltering outside heat, Jack wore his favorite blue blazer, the very one his wife purchased years ago as a wedding anniversary gift. He stood alone behind the stomach-high mesh field divider covered with metal-plated ads of local companies like "Doyle Oil" and "Tommy C's Auto Insurance."

He had recently turned 45, but few could tell. Friends thought his splendid physical condition was due to his being a seasoned New York State Trooper, but he knew better.

Simply, it was because of the daily scheduled physical workouts with his teenage son, Patrick. Six foot two inches tall, consistently weighing 190 pounds, with a full head of slightly graying hair, many commented he resembled James Garner's "Rockford Files" character when dressed in standard detective attire; blazer, white collared button-down shirt minus a tie, or during the summer a white polo shirt, khaki pants, dark fedora and his trusted, issued .357 holstered diligently, attached to his always black belt.

Jack was certain others wondered why he attended every high school baseball game, since he had no vested interest in the team or outcome. It was difficult to explain, but he was drawn to this sport like loose change to a magnet. Being present temporarily soothed the constant ache in his heart, he surmised.

He watched the hustling varsity players, then glanced at the newly installed electric scoreboard in right field, which indicated the visiting

Kingston team at bat, was down by a run in the bottom of the seventh and it was the last inning. Jack remembered if not for the financial efforts of Bob Cohen, the founding partner of a local renown ambulance-chasing litigating law firm, the school district would still be utilizing the former archaic score panel, the one requiring several volunteers to manually update game information inning-by-inning, batter-by-batter, pitch-by-pitch. He also discerned, albeit cynically, Bob had ensured a logo of his law firm be prominently placed dead center on the board.

Cynicism aside, it also informed Jack the present batter had no strikes and three balls on the count. Lastly, he noted there were two outs. Luckily, he had arrived at the most opportune time.

The smallish, but lightning fast pitch runner, wearing a pristine white uniform, stood yards off first base. He continuously taunted the pitcher by jumping to his left and right, attempting to interrupt any concentration. Chomping on a wad of bubble gum wrapped around inexpensive chewing tobacco, the pitcher eyed him with evident disdain. The fans, now all stood, increasing the volume of their cheering. Jack joined in, enthusiastically, but softly, absently touching his secured fire arm.

The pitcher, with acne-covered cheeks, seldom cared about the opinions of his compact catcher, thinking they were irrelevant. He shook off the squatting teammate's numerous hand signals, before nodding in agreement to the next pitch selection. As he began the wind-up, the pitcher suddenly fired a pick-off throw to first.

Clearly, the annoying, goading, speedy runner was ill-prepared and narrowly reached the bag. He slowly picked himself up off the infield dirt, wiping away dusty remnants from the soiled jersey. Dispirited, and having lost the inclination to steal second, he tentatively stepped off the bag, no longer wanting to test the testy pitcher.

Ready for battle, the tall hurler smiled condescendingly at the now subdued opponent, allowing him to redirect his attention back toward his waiting teammate, who kept fidgeting with the too tight-fitting chest guard. He began the next pitch while the crowd shouted last chance encouragements.

Not willing to be the beneficiary of his opponent's guff, the winning-run batter, in an unorthodox coiled stance, took a hefty cut at a fastball, but missed, causing him to twist into a pretzel-like shape before falling to the ground. Embarrassed, he stepped back into the box, and superstitiously banged the silver aluminum bat against both cleats three times.

Seemingly confident in his own playing skills, the young batter nervously glanced over his shoulder at someone in the visiting stands. The veteran detective sensed that that someone was the particularly loud, screaming adult, whose uneven facial stubble was pressed against the backstop. Wearing a worn New York Yankees tank top barely covering his expansive beer gut, Jack noted the colorless prison-like tattoos running the length of both arms.

It was the player's father, Jack deduced. He immediately sized up the atavistic weathered-looking, rictus-faced individual. Jack concluded he was the typical overly talkative, aggressive parent who overcompensated for past physical shortcomings through the athletic accomplishments of an offspring.

Unfortunately, Jack had seen too many of these wannabes during his rookie year on the force. When working as a uniformed officer, he was frequently summoned to break up brawls between intoxicated male patrons at local taverns. They would typically wear overpriced T-shirts, jackets and caps of their selected favorite professional teams, while watching them battle on televised events. These same combatants spent money on highly marked-up beer and hard liquor, which would have undoubtedly been better expended on their emotionally deprived families who waited in physically neglected houses or, more likely than not, trailers.

The slugger looked away from his irate dad, feeling the confidence ebb at this crucial time. He attempted to intently focus on the pitcher, who looked even taller while standing on the mound. The ace spat a dark stream of tobacco juice at the direction of the batter, wiping away the watery residue from his chin with an ancient mitt.

He swung hard and efficiently at the next pitch. Making contact, the ball exploded high into the air. Every player, on the field and in the dugouts alike, froze, watching the arching ball. Even the screaming idiot father became unexpectedly still.

The centerfielder, distracted by a swarm of pesky mosquitoes, had inadvertently moved closer to the infield. He momentarily hesitated after hearing the crack of the bat. Looking up, he became initially blinded by the partially setting sun. But the flummoxed boy, to his dismay, quickly realized the ball was headed toward him. Suddenly, the ill-prepared player turned and raced in the direction of Jack.

Uncertain of the ball's destination, the young boy feared his bug preoccupation would prevent him from catching the object. Wishing now he had paid closer attention to the game, the outfielder ran at full speed toward where he anticipated, actually prayed, the baseball would land, diving at the last second. As his body crashed onto the waiting warning track, the ball magically landed in the open glove. Except for the sound of passing wayward seagulls heading for scraps at a nearby fast food restaurant garbage dumpster, an eerie silence engulfed the field and stands.

The player stood up, ball in hand, raising it in the air. An overweight umpire chugged in the direction from second base, losing his cap in the process. Seeing the clutched ball, he hollered, "Out."

The home team went wild, charging to the centerfielder. The crowd erupted while the batter and runner stared in disbelief. The young boy, now an unexpected star, held the ball tightly in his fist.

"That's my boy," said Jack, excitedly.

The elated youth turned back toward the lone man. "What's that, mister?" he asked, beginning to absorb the adulation.

"Uh, nice catch, son," he corrected himself to the smiling player who was quickly tackled and swarmed by jubilant teammates.

Looking back at the visitors' stands, Jack could still vaguely hear the hot-headed father's looping rants to whoever would listen. After several seconds, the State Trooper painstakingly began trekking back to his waiting, tainted, Ford Falcon Wagon.

§§§§

Near dinner time, numerous high school seniors milled about, chatting on a sprawling backyard that gently sloped to the wide Hudson River. It was the unofficial and unsupervised kick-off party for the class of 1985. Most potential graduates appeared to be in attendance with borrowed automobiles from unwitting parents. The cars were parked in front of near identical, nondescript ranch and split-level homes nestled on a long, winding street feeding a lonely cul-de-sac.

The waters were unusually calm as groups of students stood near the shoreline watching refuse-filled barges being guided down the brownish silk current by an over-achieving, chugging tugboat. One student, wearing thick eyeglasses, lobbed a ragged tennis ball into the river for an ecstatic Irish Setter, who swam, fetched, and returned the soggy object in its slobbering mouth, eager for another round.

The picnic tables located near the newly constructed wooden back deck were loaded with various bowls of chips and dips. Next to these, but closer to the sliding glass door leading into the kitchen, sat a large keg of beer resting in a tub of ice. A refill keg sat close by – waiting. The partygoers dressed in various summer attire, danced together, some kissing, to a blaring Huey Lewis song.

Patrick sat alone, away from the revelers, in a flimsy, plaid lawn chair watching his fellow classmates. Despite being popular, he often felt out of place at these types of social settings. He somehow associated himself with the different cliques without becoming a member of any. He was not a drinker, nor did he smoke pot or experiment with other drugs. He did not play on any organized sporting team, and except for student government, he did not participate in after-school programs, like the drama or music programs. With the exception of being class president during all three years of high school, Patrick kept to himself, spending time teaching himself to play the guitar. He emotionally removed himself from most student-related activities in pursuit of a more personal goal.

Looking to his left, suspended between two enormous pine trees, was an unrecognizable couple, clumsily making out on a portable sun-bleached hammock. To his right, in an identical lawn chair, sat Desi, his best buddy, who already displayed intemperate mannerisms. Holding a cup of beer in each hand, he carefully straightened three additional cups of beer with his mismatched Puma sneakered feet so they were in a neat and orderly line.

Patrick considered himself lucky to be friends with the guzzling companion. Recently voted the "best-looking" guy in their class, Desi also happened to be a gifted All-State football player. Between the looks and athletic notoriety, meeting girls was a non-issue. But for all his accomplishments, Desi was probably the most insecure person he knew. To mask shortcomings, he was merciless with other classmate's imperfections – his comments could be biting, at best, and fortunately, never directed at Patrick.

In fact, the handsome athlete was his guardian angel of sorts. Since Patrick did not drive, Desi would always pick him up in the hand-me-down sky blue Skylark he inherited from his older brother, Rory. He also ensured the two attended as many parties and school outings together.

Since infancy, Patrick and Desi grew up just houses away from one another. Their parents had become fast friends after Jack relocated the family to this small upstate town. Although not related, they both referred to the respective parents as "Aunt" and "Uncle."

Most times, the two were basically joined at the hip. In fact, Desi was with him on that momentous day ten years ago. They complemented each other, so Patrick would like to think, though he was never quite certain what he brought to their friendship table.

He doubted his buddy really understood anything about him or the daily struggles he encountered during the past decade. Patrick thought he had a handle on his fellow students because it was his nature to be curious, and besides, he was a unique listener. Unlike him, most guys in his grade were usually girl- and status-driven.

Yes, Patrick actually enjoyed asking and learning about different people, but not in a prying way or with gossipy intentions. He was genuinely concerned about the well-being of others. Perhaps he was more sensitive, if not too sensitive, about those less fortunate. And he had a knack for making people feel immediately comfortable when in his company.

Recently, he became conscious about classmates rarely reciprocating with inquiries, especially male counterparts. Patrick was unsure if it was because of immaturity, selflessness, or simply a lack of interest. He sensed a growing weariness in typical one-way conversations and began questioning what was gained from them. Quite simply, Patrick wished for a similar listener.

Desi motioned to the couple making out. "Kevin's not doing so badly with Lori," he said.

"I guess," Patrick replied, gripping his thighs.

Patrick looked over at Kevin, the high school's starting quarterback, who had his hand up the back of Lori's faded jean shirt. "Get a motel room, man," said Desi.

Kevin responded by giving the favorite wide receiver the middle finger, continuing to move his other hand up and down her back.

Desi elbowed Patrick. "Man, I am hornier than a motherfucker," he said frustratingly, scratching newly sprouted chin whiskers.

Patrick looked up and saw Kim, a Chinese-born girl from school, saunter toward them wearing a red and white polka-dotted halter. Excluding her younger sister, she was the only Asian student in their district. Actually, her family was the single Asian family in town who happened to own a chain of dry cleaning stores around the Mid-Hudson Valley.

Without saying hello to either, she took a lone cup of the cheap beer from Desi, drinking the contents in one continuous swallow. She then nonchalantly dropped the empty cup to the lawn, seductively wiping her lips with an extraordinarily long, spiky tongue.

"Hey," she slurred, while running both hands through chemically induced, curly black hair.

Instinctive reflexes caused Desi to jump up, though too hastily, spilling the three remaining cups of beer on the ground. He took hold of Kim's slender arm, walking away. He turned to Patrick, slapping a five on the exposed hand.

"Wanna learn some moves?" he asked, taking one last gulp of the warm flat beer.

Patrick's attention, no longer on Desi, had focused on the guy using the wheelchair. Dennis was popping wheelies and flirting outrageously with a group of girls. He was a past high school graduate, sporting an uncommon crew cut. Having flunked out of Fordham the previous academic year, he was informing his captive audience he was taking "a year off" to travel the country in a recently purchased, battered, orange VW Beetle.

Patrick whispered a soliloquy to himself, "I gotta get laid."

He sipped Pepsi from a can, using a waxed paper straw. The warm weather caused the narrow tube to wilt and collapse forcing him to suck even harder for the sugary beverage to reach waiting lips. A petite, alluring blonde girl lazily approached holding a coffee mug with an out-of-place inscription "Mom of the Year" in one hand and a glass milk bottle filled with a red substance in the other.

"Want some?" she asked.

"What is it?"

"Vodka and something," the petite blond said, attempting to sound sober.

Patrick enjoying the instant attention, declined the mystery beverage and continued unsuccessfully to suck any cola. After several moments, he looked up to discover the attractive girl watching with a confused look.

"No thanks," he said, finally giving up on the straw, tossing it toward an overflowing, cracked plastic garbage pail.

"C'mon, it's a party," she protested, smiling tenderly.

Taking a sip of her drink, she lost her balance falling onto his lap. He was fortunate to catch and steady the girl, annoyingly dropping the soda in the process, as she shakily stood upright.

"I don't drink," Patrick remarked, cautiously.

Finally in control of balance issues, but yet feeling terribly tired, she sat on his legs. "Too bad," she stated, somewhat matter-of-factly.

With her resting on his knees, Patrick could observe an incredible body complementing striking good looks. The tube-top contrasted nicely with her endowed tanned chest and shoulders, acid washed jeans, and bare feet. As she poured more red liquid into the mug, some kids walked by, waving and greeting him, but not stopping.

"Pat-trick," one yelled.

Taking a sip of her mixed drink, the petite blond looked at the yeller, then at him. "Your name's Patrick?" she repeated, too loudly. "I'm Penny. That's soooo funny. Patrick and Penny."

It suddenly occurred to him it was peculiar he did not recognize this flirting female. "Who are you?" he finally asked curiously, already fancying her. "I've never seen you at school."

"I go to Bishop Dunne," the girl laughed, as he looked beyond, wondering if anyone was spying the exchange.

"The all-girls school," Patrick said, flattered by the unsolicited affection, as she unexpectedly began tussling his hair.

Not long ago, the neighboring towns supported four Catholic high schools, but over time, because of fiscal realities, three closed, one by one. The prime properties were sold by the Archdiocese to real estate developers for hefty profits, leaving Bishop Dunne as the lone Catholic educational offering. Because it shared space with an active convent on a still well-maintained campus, it remained a single-sex school for women.

"I can't stand going there," she said, annoyed.

"Wouldn't bother me," he said, reaching to touch the hand twirling his wavy brown hair.

"I bet it wouldn't," Penny teased, giving him a warm look, she finished the remaining contents in the ceramic container.

"What happened to him?" she asked, letting go of Patrick's hand, pointing at Dennis who was performing dips from the wheelchair.

"You don't know?" he said, filtering information while taking the empty mug, placing it next to the lawn chair.

She shook her head no, but was clearly interested.

"That's Dennis'" he remarked in a matter-of-fact way. "He graduated from high school two years ago. He was the class clown."

"But what happened to him?" Penny asked with a downcast look. "Was he born like that?"

He paused, puzzled to see if there was an ulterior motive behind the interest. Realizing it was genuine, he continued.

"No," Patrick said. "He was in the military. A Cadet at West Point, actually."

"So he got hurt in a war or something?" Penny asked, perplexed but transfixed on the wheelchair-using guy.

"It happened during the Beirut crisis," his eyes only on his companion, attracted to the sensitivity echoing from her words. "But he was in Panama."

"Why Panama?" she pestered, casting a glance before boldly looking back at Dennis.

"See, the Army had its seasoned Marines in Lebanon, so they sent the young Cadets like him to fill in at the different embassies," he remarked.

Penny said nothing at first. She looked down, at Dennis, and then finally back at Patrick. "He got shot?" she asked. "Or stepped on a mine, huh?"

Patrick was not certain if her eyes were watering, but he made the conscious decision to finish the story, for better or worse.

"He got drunk and fell into the Canal," he answered, wondering if he should wipe the tears slowly streaking down her soft cheeks.

He unsuccessfully looked around for a napkin. "You're kidding?" she whispered, wanting to extract additional information.

"Ask him," he said, pausing, desperately eager to change the subject to snap her out of this unexpectedly dejected state.

Penny could not take her gaze away from Dennis as he was wheeled around the lawn by two friends, one on each back push handle. "That's terrible," she said innocently. "He's such a good-looking guy."

Surprising them both, Patrick almost shoved her off, an angry look crossing his face. "If he was ugly it'd be okay that he's paralyzed?" he challenged in a surly tone. "What difference does that make?"

"I'm only saying," she stammered, politely.

He quickly realized that although he had snapped Penny out of the depressive mood, he had inadvertently caused her to become surprisingly defensive. He grasped to save the moment.

"It's just that he's my best friend," Patrick said with added dramatic affect in his voice. "I'm still not over his accident. Dennis always wanted to be a soldier."

She said nothing at first, but there was a look between them. He understood he had in fact, salvaged the exchange. Biting a plump lower lip, and holding his hand again, Penny stood, with obvious prurient thoughts, attempting to pull him up.

"Wanna take a walk?" she asked.

"Walk?" he choked, letting go to hold onto the lawn chair armrests. "Now? Where?"

Penny giggled nodding toward the woods, grabbing his left arm tugging hard to free him from a sitting position. "You know," she coyly said.

All air seemed to have escaped his flashing hot lungs. Feeling faint, he looked at her, almost pleadingly. "Oh, yeah, well," Patrick said, balking.

But before he could finish responding, a voice shouted a name from the back deck. It was Jimmy, the classmate hosting the party.

"Patrick," he yelled. "Your dad's here."

Patrick looked over his shoulder, spotting the figure that caused his face to turn as white as the knuckles now embedded in the lawn chair armrests. Standing next to Jimmy, who was unsuccessfully attempting to block the view of the stainless steel kegs, was Jack Flannery, still wearing the blue blazer.

Jack was clearly upset at the teens' drinking as he witnessed a young girl race by, cupping her mouth while vomit trickled through her fingers. Being both a State Trooper and parent got the best of him. He was apt to call Jimmy's absent parents this instant, but he chose a different path.

"That's not beer in your cup, Jimmy, is it?" he inquired accusingly.

Jimmy, built like the brick house heavyweight wrestler he was, had a woebegone look and could not decide if he should run after the puking girl, who he could see through the open sliding glass door, her head in the kitchen sink, or stay and try to keep Detective Flannery distracted.

"No, no, Mr. Flannery," the culprit said, failing to give the respect befitted a veteran decorated law enforcement official. "It's, it's ginger ale."

"Right," Jack responded angrily to the obvious lie. "Load the kegs and any other alcohol into the back of my car – now. I'll make sure to speak with your parents when they return to thank them for letting you host this party."

Not wanting to create a controversy, a fearful Jimmy concluded it was incumbent upon him to calm down the near enraged off-duty officer. It clearly took precedent over the puking girl.

Firstly, Mr. Flannery was known to everyone as a no-nonsense kind of person. Yes, nice, as parents go, but someone who did not tolerate his imposed value lines being crossed. Secondly, vomit was a temporary problem. The stench may remain for a while, but it could be cleaned up.

His parents on the other hand, were a potentially longer-term concern. He knew they would be irate after learning of this ill-conceived party during their Boston weekend vacation. Any punishment, he knew, would be swift, harsh and without debate. Jimmy already calculated the probable loss of driving privileges would interfere with a date he had lined up with Dawn Diaz at next month's homecoming dance.

"Yes, sir," Jimmy, obediently agreed.

Jack looked toward his son. "Come on," he barked. "Mass starts in 20 minutes. Then we have to work out."

Patrick was at a loss, the ruse over. Any chance with Penny was now ruined by the arrival of his father. After a tenuous moment between this girl, Dennis wheeled up.

"Here you go," Dennis said, cheerfully. "Good luck in the hospital tomorrow."

Dennis stood up from the wheelchair and stepped away. Instinctively, Patrick drew the chair toward him, securely locking the brakes and slid into it. Hooking his right arm underneath both knees, he pulled. Reaching down, Patrick secured his heels in the foot rest, finally straightening the wheelchair cushion.

A leg began to unexpectedly vibrate, though, causing him to tame the vicious spasm by squeezing a calf. Patrick turned back to Penny, who was staring, dumbstruck. He tried flashing a killer-cute smile.

"A miracle?" he said lamely.

Realizing what had just taken place, Dennis laughed at the perverse joke and walked away. Speechless, Penny could not believe what had just occurred. Was this the first time he pulled this type of prank? And why do this to her? Was she simply at the wrong place at the wrong time? Penny knew she was a prize and could have any guy, but she had begun tiring of high school jocks and the baggage they seem to carry. Even with being tipsy, she sensed, if only for a short time, that Patrick might be different. But this seemingly nice guy played and included her in a cruel hoax.

She was wronged and humiliated.

Without hesitation, she slapped Patrick across the face, storming off.

Patrick lost the killer-cute smile.

§§§§

The Flannery family arrived late to the Saturday 5:30 Mass. Jack drove, his wife Agnes shared the front vinyl bench seat, while Patrick occupied the back with his sixteen year-old sister, Dana. His father was strict about numerous things, and punctuality was a top five. Yet, every week without fail, the family scrambled, rarely making religious services on time.

His father pulled their auto into the church's single designated handicapped parking space, located next to a side entrance, near the back of the church. The spot with the bent blue and white international wheelchair symbol sign – damaged by an errant plow after a Nor'easter snowstorm the previous winter. This entrance was the only wheelchair-accessible one, and even that was stretching the definition of the word "accessible." One needed to navigate a steep ramp that had been constructed when the chapel's interior was refurbished four years earlier, making it easier for construction workers to transport materials and rubble in and out during an extensive facelift project. When the work was complete, the parish opted to keep the ramp for the growing elderly church-going population who attended Masses both daily and weekly, as well as for the ancient Cullen twins who recently celebrated their 50th Anniversary as the clerical maintenance men.

Jack lifted his son's wheelchair from the back, which was competing for space with the confiscated kegs, pushing it toward Patrick's open door. While he made the physical maneuver from the auto to his chair, mom, dad and sister scampered away, entering the old church without him via the inaccessible front main doors with the other tardy parishioners, leaving him to enter O sole mio.

Once successfully completing the transfer, Patrick closed the car door behind him, proceeding up the shoddily constructed sloped surface. After reaching the landing-less top, he pulled open the exterior, heavy, wooden Gothic door, and in one tricky, well-practiced motion, cleared the wheelchair out of the way, without rolling back down the incline.

This seldom-used entry led directly into a long, narrow storage room directly off the altar. Candles of innumerable size and color, with an overwhelming waxy aroma, were stacked from floor to ceiling, making the area difficult to traverse. To actually access the interior pews, Patrick was required to wheel onto the altar, separated from this room by a thick, red wine-colored velvet curtain. Peeking out, he sensed the opening Mass song was ending.

Like a vast majority of the parish, his parents preferred this popular Mass because it was the designated folk version. Patrick cryptically thought it was a vain attempt for some to feel "hip" or "with-it" by attending.

On any given Saturday, six or seven young aspiring musicians played guitars, flutes, tambourines, and different types of drums, while an equal number simply sang in the makeshift chorus. The band's attire was a combination of the '60s meeting the '80s. The guys, with their sideburns a tad too long and their mousse-saturated, highlighted and probably flammable hair, pushed the sleeves of their pastel-colored, cotton sports coats up both forearms, while the female members seemed to have squeezed into too-tight, dark designer jeans, with loose fitting blouses unbuttoned one button lower than necessary.

"In the name of the father, the son, and...," the elderly Monsignor announced dogmatically, following a few seconds of silence.

Patrick utterly dreaded attending Mass. Forgetting the inaccessibility issues and the personal growing ambivalence with Catholicism, his family's continual tardiness caused a degree of humiliation. Every seven days he was forced to make this unintentional entrance. Disturbed, he hesitated, took a deep breath before rolling in, for all to observe, like the Broadway star actor making his grand, Act One appearance.

§§§§

The Monsignor, who had grown used to this ritual, calmly stopped for the young wheelchair user, mouthing a "hello" with a pleasant countenance. Perched in front of his sedile high above the altar, he peered down on all followers. Patrick looked at the other, much junior priest sitting at the religious leader's right side, albeit lower, who offered a warm, friendly nod. The altar boys waved, as did the entire folk band for that matter, as if on cue.

The second part of the entrance scenario caused additional angst. There was one riser separating the elevated altar from the building's pews. To Patrick's chagrin, the Parish Council never corrected this access slight. So instead, he dealt with this six-inch obstacle in front of 1,000 curious eyes, with unexplainable fascination, as he circumnavigated this designated solitary route.

Patrick positioned his wheelchair in order to properly pop a wheelie off the tiered level. Unexplainably, this week he rushed, misjudging the maneuver on recently polished, ornate patterned marble floor. This error caused the wheelchair to land irregularly, pitching him forward, practically ejecting Patrick. As the churchgoers gasped, two guitar players leapt to assist. One grabbed the chair, allowing the other to grasp Patrick's upper body.

"Getting rusty?" the Monsignor joked, receiving the expected respectful laughter from his flock. Patrick looked out at the fellow parishioners, then back at the younger priest who could only shrug.

"And let us all pray for our own Speed Racer," the Monsignor continued. "This dear young boy will again be entering St. Jude's tomorrow and I'm confident he'll finally come out walking again this year."

The Monsignor picked-up where he left off. "...and the Holy Spirit, Amen," hearing only snatches of the recited prayer, a humiliated Patrick, his head lowered, flew down the center aisle completing the journey to his sanctuary at the rearmost part of the church.

§§§§

Following Mass, the religious community milled outside in different sub-groups, between the red brick house of worship and Craftsman-style rectory. Patrick was sitting next to the younger priest, Jack conversed separately with the Monsignor, Dana hung with a small group of teenage girlfriends, and Mrs. Flannery gossiped with other mothers, nearby.

"I will never live down his accident until he is out of that damn wheelchair," Jack Flannery exclaimed too emphatically, causing the elderly cleric to instinctively give the sign-of-the-cross.

"Sorry, Monsignor," he said, ashen-face. "I did not mean to swear."

Patrick was intrigued by Catholic nuances and idiosyncrasies. This parish, Blessed Sacrament, was spiritually led by Monsignor Keane, who everyone liked, but rarely saw. Keane was raised in a wealthy Bronxville family who bequeathed a trust, enabling him to annually flip for a new Mercedes auto. The Monsignor, now in his early 70s, was quite tall, but bent, lean and strangely, missing several front bottom teeth. Patrick could not help but stare at the dark gap whenever Keane smiled. The Monsignor had developed a quirky habit of constantly wiping off white dandruff flakes from his freshly pressed jet-black shirt or stiffly dry cleaned coat. Yes, the church seemed well-run, but Patrick frequently doubted Keane was active in the day-to-day decisions, since the pristine luxury car was often missing from the prominent parking space reserved specifically for him immediately outside the rectory's spacious sun room.

Beneath Keane in parish ranking, was the middle-aged priest, Father John Gorman. He was a spoiled, portly sort, with ever-present sweaty palms, who appeared to expect the many trappings characteristically bestowed most spiritual leaders. The man enjoyed having his meals cooked, clothes laundered, white collars bleached and heavily starched, as well as receiving constant invitations to local country clubs for golf outings and dinners. In return, his sermons tended to be short, bland, meandering, lacking themes or messages. Fr. Gorman provided meager religious guidance. Although at least fifteen years younger than the Monsignor, Gorman's pasty appearance made him look senior. Patrick concluded he became a member of the cloth for all the wrong reasons, which only clouded the teenager's affinity to the Catholic Church.

The low cleric on the totem pole was Father O'Sullivan, a recent New York Archdiocese Seminary graduate. Dashing, articulate, charismatic, and liberal, the Archbishop stationed him to Blessed Sacrament for his exemplary bilingual skills. In an act of enlightenment, before being ordained, the Archbishop sent several seminarians to Puerto Rico for a six-month Spanish immersion program, believing this would enable the new clerics to better communicate with the burgeoning Hispanic Catholic population. One mandate dictated the rookie priests host weekly Spanish-speaking Masses for recent immigrants.

To no one's surprise, Fr. O'Sullivan was an immediate hit with the vast number of church members, as well as an instant celebrity within the Hispanic community. Clearly, his fealty to the religion was unquestionable. The priest found himself in high demand for family dinners, weddings, communions, as well as funerals and burials. Local black Baptist churches and Jewish Synagogues would rely on him to support their particular civil or religious causes and fundraisers. Politicians also depended on his guidance whenever racial disturbances erupted yearly at the local high school. Often, the priest could be found playing pick-up basketball games in public parks or the church's gymnasium, with kids either attending CYO or who simply lived in the surrounding, blighted neighborhood.

Fr. O'Sullivan was the sole conduit Patrick had with his evaporating faith. He found the cleric to regularly prod, requiring deep reflection of the soul when discussing spiritual, social and racial problems. These conversations forced the student to conclude life was not simplistic. It was not black or white as he once thought, but instead, many shades of gray.

In the meantime, Mrs. Flannery was still sequestered with the other women. Predictably, Patrick was the focus of this group's interaction, too.

"I'm worried about all the pressure on my son," Mrs. Flannery informed them, intentionally trying not to sound alarmed. "He's so focused on making his father proud."

"But I'm worried about Jack, too," she continued. "I just think his expectations for Patrick might be a tad unrealistic."

Not a single woman objected or disputed her assessment. In fact, their body language indicated they concurred. After discussing the topic for several more minutes, they slowly began gathering up respective family members before eventually departing for Saturday dinner rituals.

Jack was still conversing with the Monsignor, getting needed spiritual support for the upcoming week. "Thanks for the words of encouragement at Mass," he said. "As God is my witness, one day my boy will be walking in this church entrance."

"But what if by chance he doesn't, Jack?" the Monsignor dug. "Will you be able to accept God's will?"

"God's will?" he responded, incredulously without thinking. "What does that mean? The God I believe in would never allow my son to spend the rest of his life using a wheelchair."

Jack's unplanned tirade prevented him from seeing the shocked expression evident on the Monsignor's face, but before the elder could reply, Mrs. Flannery called out to her husband. Jack repositioned himself and saw Dana, Patrick, and his wife standing next to the wagon.

"I have a greater calling right now, Monsignor," he said, excusing himself. "We'll see you next week."

He vigorously clasped the religious leader's hand before heading toward his family.

§§§§

Patrick was prone on the sturdy bench press table. The black leather upholstery was tattered from overuse. It was positioned in the center of the carless double bay garage. Four lines of suspended, bright florescent lights buzzed like approaching bumble bees, casting bizarre shades between the iron ceiling beams. His sister, Dana, needing to do something to feel actively participating, held tightly onto his legs as he strained to lift the heavy barbell, while Jack unnecessarily shouted the number count.

Working out with his father was an eternal psychological game. Yes, Patrick generally enjoyed the camaraderie it provided, but he was honestly not a fan of the exercise portion. No, he thought again, who was he kidding? He hated the relentless physical therapy. He found himself making up mental scenarios to assist in surviving the five sets of innumerable exercise repetitions his dad demanded during the circadian weight-lifting routines.

Sometimes Patrick would pretend he earned $1,000 for each successful lift. He would then multiply $1,000 with every performed pump, pull, lift or dip so after a particular exercise was finished, he had accumulated additional funds in an imaginary offshore bank account. This "game" made him fictionally wealthy at the conclusion of workout sessions and even wealthier at the end of every week.

Other times he envisioned Susan Long, the captain of the high school cheerleading squad, the girl of his out-of-reach dreams, would be watching the excruciating regimen. These imagines pushed him harder to finish each drill with her impressed, make-believe beaming smile cemented in his brain.

To some, probably many, these cerebral vacations would be construed as silly, even immature, but they got Patrick through his daily physical drudgery. And how could someone know what he was thinking, anyway? Regardless, he kept the fantasies to himself.

"Come on, one more," his father said, more commanding than encouraging.

"You can do it," Dana joined in, caught up in the enthusiasm.

"You want to walk again, don't you?" Jack challenged.

Patrick grimaced, finding the willpower to lock his arms straight up. Consumed by fatigue, he collapsed, crashing the weights on the bar holder, causing the bench to shake, a loud clanging echoed in the garage.

His father slapped him on his sweaty chest. "Atta boy," Jack Flannery said, pleased and impressed. "Another set?"

"No way," he said gasping to catch his breath. "I'm spent."

Jack looked disapprovingly at his son when Dana went to retrieve the wheelchair. She placed it next to the bench table, holding it for her brother, his arms trembling during the transfer.

"Spent?" Jack said annoyed. "What does that mean? Bet you wouldn't be spent if you had skipped Jimmy's party."

"Dad, I'm beat," he conceded, desiccated and looking for a misplaced water bottle.

"You're sounding like a quitter to me," his father said, chagrined, not letting up. "This is no time to be a quitter."

Normally, Patrick was reticent and resigned himself to his father's snipes, but he was sensitive to the criticism nonetheless and was growing weary of them. "When have I ever quit?" he said, angered at the absurd comment.

When Mrs. Flannery entered the garage, Patrick continued glaring at his father. Standing close to the kitchen doorway which connected the house and car port, she sensed tension between them, per usual, and immediately tried diffusing.

"Hurry up and come eat dinner," she said, wiping her hands on a flowery designed washcloth. "The pizza was delivered five minutes ago."

He brusquely wheeled out to the driveway through the open garage doors. Mrs. Flannery tilted her head disapprovingly, looking at her husband, before returning to dinner. Trying to ignore the brewing hostilities, Dana picked a dirty towel off the immaculate garage floor. Obviously concerned, she wanted to talk about harboring fears. Just 18 months younger than Patrick, she never stopped worrying. Not that there was a reason to, really. He was good-looking, in some ways more popular than she in school, and almost too perfect to be true. Dana knew her brother was protective of his little sister, maybe a tad overly protective, but not overbearing. She considered Patrick as everyone's All-American, who just happened to use a wheelchair.

A bohemian at heart, Dana let her straight auburn hair grow long. She favored shopping at used clothing stores in Woodstock for out-of-style, loose-fitting flowered linen blouses and frayed bell-bottom jeans in perpetual need of patches. Fair skinned and beautiful, she in return shielded the older bro, whenever possible.

"What if he fails, Dad?" she asked, uneasily. "What if he doesn't walk again? Isn't this his last chance?"

Jack would admit that lately, similar thoughts crept into his mind. He understood the odds, but he could not look at this particular hospital visit in those terms. It sounded defeatist. A word, he reminded himself, which was once vacant in his vocabulary.

He unexpectedly turned on Dana. "How can you even think such a terrible thing, young lady?" he snapped.

"So you think I'm a quitter, Dad?" Patrick demanded, coming to Dana's defense. "Since my freaking accident, my life has been about me walking again. Every day I wake up, do physical therapy, go to school, and afterwards, do more physical therapy."

"You know I don't like talking about your accident," Jack said, deflecting.

But this time, the son would not let the father off the hook. "Yeah, and what's up with that?" he challenged. "You don't know anything about what it's really like for me using a wheelchair."

"Don't start with me," Jack yelled, after his son rolled toward the kitchen entrance.

Patrick stopped and turned before entering. "Don't start?" he replied in disbelief. "Well, what can I talk about? Can I talk about if I'm not strong enough again? Shit, can I talk about 'what if'?"

His father stood several feet away, dumbfounded. "Hey, young man," he said, sensing a loss of any semblance of authority. "Watch your language. I'm still your father. You will be strong enough this time. You just have to pray and believe."

"Pray and believe?" he replied, now exasperated. "You're kidding, right? Those leg braces weigh over 60 pounds. I've never been able to walk more than five feet with all the weight covering my legs."

"But we have everyone praying for you this year," Jack quickly countered.

Mrs. Flannery had been worriedly listening to the confrontation escalate. "It's true, Patrick," she said, interrupting while pulling the reheated pepperoni pizza from the oven, resting it on the cold stove burners. "The O'Hara family even gave us water from Lourdes they picked up on their summer trip to France. All you need to do is rub it on your legs every night in the hospital."

"What about New York water, Dad?" he asked, pushing himself up to the kitchen sink, grabbing a juice glass, filling it with tap water, before dumping the clear liquid over his legs, saturating the sweatpants.

"Isn't that good enough?"

"Who do you think you are, Patrick Gerard Flannery?" his father demanded, stunned but taking a threatening step forward.

Patrick gave pause. He knew lines were crossed whenever his parents used middle names. Jack reddened, but ceased ranting. Both refused to yield. Finally, his father grabbed two pieces of sizzling pizza, putting it on a flimsy paper plate, causing it to perilously sag in the middle. He then twisted off the beer bottle cap, taking a long, hard guzzle. In a huff, Patrick wheeled away from the family, heading down the hallway toward the bedrooms.

Mr. Flannery shouted after him. "I would be grounding your backside, young man, if you weren't going into the hospital tomorrow," he bluffed, reclaiming authority. "The way you've been talking back to us and using profanity in front of your mother is disgraceful."

"Leave him be, honey," his wife said, pleading.

"Yeah, give him space," Dana joined in, who was picking strands of burnt melted, mozzarella remnants off the pizza pan.

Jack spoke out to no one, everyone. "What's with this attitude," he said in a too loud of a voice. "It's not like this is his first time going into St. Jude's. I've been working with him on his physical therapy every day since his accident. I don't deserve this."

He looked first at his daughter, then wife, folding the larger slice. Jack took a hearty bite of the still hot pie, burning the top of his mouth, but was too proud to display the physical and emotional pain he felt. The patriarch headed toward the living room, wiping the warm oil from his mouth with the back of a hand, knowing for the first time Patrick had successfully fought him to a draw.

"There better be something good on TV tonight," he said to himself.

§§§§

The time on the Sony bed stand clock flipped to read 9:10 AM. Patrick was attempting, with little success, to close his overly stuffed green duffle bag. When he reached mid-point, he determined the zipper would proceed no further. Reaching into the canvas container, he began reassessing the inventory by unloading items needing to be weeded out: magazines, extra pairs of underwear, a large bag of Peanut M&M's, Hostess cakes, Wise potato chips, other goodies and several six packs of soda. He inspected the merchandise, laying them next to each other on the bed.

This decision required little contemplation. The underwear was declared expendable. He picked up the magazines, the numerous candy packets, and other items making the cut, cramming them back into the bag. With one final thrust, he pulled hard, finally closing the bursting-at-the-seams canvas duffle. Patrick could feel the annual anxiety renewing itself. As much as he would try to convince himself this hospital visit was no different than any other, he truly understood the implications of what was at stake. But forgetting the importance of this particular stay, he simply despised the hospital. It was not so much the poor food options, blood-giving, X-ray taking, doctor-poking stuff – he understood the program protocol. It was the loss of independence associated with admittance.

After nine consecutive visits, he had developed a bond with a vast majority of the nurses, physicians, therapists, and even custodial staff. However, once he traveled through the hospital entrance, his identity morphed into the number typed on the issued blue wristband. It was like being court marshaled, where the guilty were stripped of any remaining dignity.

But putting the tenseness aside, admittedly, there was something uniquely cocoon-like about the particular hospital room, reserved for teenagers, he had occupied on the pediatric floor the past four years; it had transformed into a temporary comfort zone.

Patrick lifted the guitar case, placing it on his lap. He then heaved the weighted luggage, resting it precariously on top. After wrapping the Walkman headset around his neck, he draped a favorite faded old denim jacket over the bag before beginning to carefully wheel out of the bedroom.

The neck of the guitar case bumped smartly against the doorway frame during the exiting, shifting the items on his lap and subsequently causing the denim jacket to fall off. Patrick tried grabbing, without success, on its downward path. When he tentatively leaned over to retrieve it from the floor, the duffle bag tumbled, too.

"Shit," he said, angry at himself for being clumsy.

He now tried to pick up the two items; first the bag, then the jacket. After once again delicately balancing the possessions, he proceeded forward. However, Patrick's case again smacked against the door, causing everything, including the guitar, to plummet from his lap this time. "Shit-fuck," he blurted, incensed.

There were a handful of things that drove Patrick crazy about using a wheelchair – about being disabled. The most frustration occurred when objects slipped from his lap or when he simply dropped things. It made him feel uncoordinated, even when that was the farthest from the truth. But it was always embarrassing, especially when around strangers who would either offer too much assistance too quickly or would curiously watch to see how this wheelchair user would fix the fix he was in. When objects fell merely inches from his reach, well that was like salt on the wound – inexplicably, he took these instances personally.

Other times, he inadvertently ran the wayward articles over when they fell while wheeling, unnaturally flattening or tattooing the item with his tire tracks. When this occurred, which seemed far too frequently, an enraged Patrick turned on himself. Perhaps this was inexplicable to the non-disabled, but it still drove him insane, nonetheless.

As much as he tried to act like using a wheelchair was no big deal or did not make him feel differently from non-wheelchair-using friends, this dropping habit was a constant reminder that he was, in fact, disabled and different.

Needless to say, Patrick wheeled around the fallen items, leaving the room and personal possessions on the bedroom floor for someone else to retrieve.

§§§§

On this smoggy, scorching day, Patrick waited on the sidewalk next to the family wagon parked outside the front hospital entry. His mother stood next to him while Jack Flannery sat behind the steering wheel. A nearby taciturn rookie city police officer, who moments before had barked for the auto to be moved away from this prime parking location citing an obscure infraction, now contritely let them be, after discovering he had unbeknownst harassed a high-ranking State Trooper. Although there was often a level of mistrust between competing law enforcement agencies, generally, rank and file cut respective law personnel slack when caught committing minor traffic infractions.

Patrick looked up and down the city block. He often wondered what the rest of Greenwich Village offered. Every year, his parents took an identical route to St. Jude's, as well as the same path home after being discharged. Patrick never explored the clearly vibrant neighborhood, which he was informed had become a haven for authentic ethnic restaurants, eclectic retail stores, and bars catering to gays, whatever that meant.

He knew his father was not a big fan of driving in Manhattan. Granted, Jack was raised in Washington Heights, but he never owned a car until moving to the suburbs following graduation from the State Police Academy. There was traffic, traffic, and more borough traffic making driving intolerable. Finding a parking spot on any street was virtually impossible, and Jack Flannery's police car "park anywhere for free" mentality detested paying the extortion-level rates the local exposed lots and garages charged.

Admittedly, Jack was anal about his automobiles. The family sedans and government-issued undercover police cruiser were all washed and waxed early every Saturday morning on their long, home driveway. And his classic, usually covered candy apple red '64 Mustang, was off-limits to all hands, except his. On the rare instances they were inadvertently nicked or God forbid, dented, it would put him in a frenzy – and paint nicks seemed to inevitably occur whenever venturing around the city.

"I'll meet you both in the lobby," he announced, noting approaching dark clouds.

"Be careful," his mother advised, apprehensively.

A forlorn Patrick bravely picked up his guitar and painstakingly wheeled on the refurbished cement path, looking like a prisoner headed to the gallows with a supportive mother trailing close behind.

§§§§

The hospital lobby was cavernous with large, ornate marble pillars and religious paintings that enhanced a secular-themed feel. The stellar medical center, founded by the Catholic Church almost a century ago, had greatly expanded and was now an edifice of buildings constructed at various times throughout the past 100 years.

Mrs. Flannery touched her son's shoulder. "I'll be right back," she said. "I just want to purchase a book for you. Wait for me right here."

Before Patrick could respond, she entered the cramped gift shop. His mother, always well-meaning, tended to buy things he would never purchase himself. Shirts, candy, it did not matter – she never seemed to hit the mark. Even purposeful directed hints about preferences had little impact on her tunnel vision. Not wanting to hurt his mom's feelings, he would graciously accept the gifts, and then either give away anything perishable or conveniently lose or misplace whatever was not.

He continued wheeling around the ill-lit hospital lobby, absorbing the familiar sights and sounds. Muzak pumped through an outdated, lobby sound system, interrupted by a crackling, heavily accented NYC female voice constantly paging needed doctors or staff. Old and young visitors carrying tropical flowers or partially deflated helium balloons, doctors carrying charts, maintenance men pushing carts, patients wearing robes and slippers wandered about in non-defined directions.

The organized chaos engulfed Patrick into a state of blankness as he placed the guitar case on an empty ligneous bench – he was now officially apprehensive. He would never admit it or let on to his parents, but there it was, he was petrified.

Unlike him, personnel and guests were free to come and go with impunity, a disposition he envied. They could eat anything they wanted, frequent movie theaters or just catch rays at a nearby community park, if desired. He, however, lost those precious rights, once admitted.

Jarring him from this preoccupation was a young, beautiful woman, wearing a breezy, aqua pantsuit, walking alone through the waiting space. She spotted Patrick, eying his guitar. The woman exited through the cafeteria doors at the same moment a medical team exploded through the emergency room pushing a stretcher, almost knocking him from the wheelchair.

He felt dizzy, the bedlam overwhelming. Through the commotion, he heard the cries of a child in the distance. The sound tunneled in the enormous atrium. Patrick searched for the screaming, finally locating it amongst the crowd. A dark-skinned toddler, naked except for the oversized, disposable diapers sliding down the child's hips, entered his vision. Thick elastic bandages tightly wrapped the little one's hands.

In a flash, a woman wearing a head-to-toe white, flowing uniform and shoes, scooped the crying boy into her arms. Patrick recognized the woman at once. Sister Margaret, an elderly nun who had tirelessly run the pediatrics floor for over twenty-five years, held the upset child, stroking his inviting cheeks. Her stern-looking face softened, the whispers transforming the cries into laughter. Patrick thought her Clorox-bleached habit seemed to glow in the darkish room.

In his opinion, Sister Margaret was as integral to the hospital complex as any of the original stained glass windows. He virtually grew up in the medical center with this woman, who seemed to be in the confines 24/7. Although she resided in a small, Spartan apartment attached to an equally barren office directly across from the elevators on Patrick's assigned floor, he knew little about her life before St. Jude's. Often Patrick wished he could inquire as to why she decided to live such an austere life requiring, in his opinion, too many personal sacrifices.

Like a priest, Sister Margaret could never marry, but unlike ordained men, she was prevented from leading a parish or Mass only because of gender. Recently, enlightened Catholics had begun allowing women to serve as Eucharistic Ministers. However, it did not prevent Patrick from believing his religion treated the sexes differently.

The familiar voices interrupted his thoughts. Looking away from the nun and boy, he saw his parents walking toward where he waited. Jack Flannery was carrying the overly stuffed duffle bag, with mom waving a polka-dotted gift shop paper bag.

"Well you're all set," his father said. "The admitting papers are signed."

"Look at the book I bought you," his mother volunteered. "I think you'll like it."

"Thanks, Mom," he replied, staring at the cover, The Hardy Boys "What Happened at Midnight."

After his father placed the duffle bag on top of his guitar case, Patrick immediately stuffed the book deeply into the canvas. "You shouldn't have. Really, really, you shouldn't have," he continued.

"Want me to get you lunch?" his father asked. "How about a cheeseburger?"

But before he could respond, a matronly woman, wearing a pink, knee-length coat, with oddly thinning bronze hair, walked out of the Admission Office, heading for the threesome. The woman resembled an old, sex-deprived, librarian. Making a beeline for Patrick and forgetting about introductions or pleasantries, the pink lady placed the standard wide, blue plastic ID bracelet around his left wrist.

Sister Margaret, noting the too businesslike manner, headed toward the Flannery family, with the squirming young boy safely in her arms. She touched Mrs. Flannery's shoulder after reaching the small group.

"Sister," his mother said. "Good to see you again."

"Mr. and Mrs. Flannery, what have you been feeding your son?" Sister Margaret raved, a tinge of an Irish brogue still evident. "I almost didn't recognize him. Patrick's practically a man."

"Yes, the weight lifting has really filled him out," Jack said, instantly bragging. "We decided he wasn't strong enough last year."

Rolling his eyes, Patrick added, "Right, we decided."

"My little man knows this is a do-or-die week," he added, pretending not to hear his son.

"What happened to this beautiful child?" Mrs. Flannery asked the nun, who continued holding the fidgeting tot.

"It's so sad," she said, reluctantly. "It's beyond comprehension. The poor little boy's miserable parents are his problem. They prey on him like animals. Just last week they were high and decided to put his tiny hands on the oven burners for fun. This is the second time he has been brought to us this year."

"You can't be serious," Mr. Flannery said, bitterly. He took the amiable child, Tito, from the nun, messing his thick hair before lifting him high into the air. "Were they arrested?"

"Yes, they both were," Sister Margaret said. "With all the endured pain in his short life, he's still the most lovable boy."

Although not wanting to interrupt the fun Tito was having, Patrick was impatient for them to leave. "Okay, you can go home now," he said with little segue.

"What?" his father said, flustered and a bit resentful. "We'll just go upstairs with you to make sure you're settled in."

The Muzak suddenly ended as the young, beautiful woman reentered the lobby, like a mirage. Patrick spotted her, this deity, in awe, speaking too loudly to himself. "I gotta get laid," he uttered, mesmerized.

It was as if time froze. Every head turned within a fifteen-foot radius after hearing this intense declaration. The young, beautiful woman also looked again at him, not losing her infectious smile. Fortunately, the Muzak again continued playing through the hidden speakers.

"We can bring your son upstairs," the feisty nun said, still covering Tito's ears. "He'll be fine."

The off-duty trooper reluctantly handed Tito back to her. "Sister, are you sure?" he offered.

"Patrick's been doing this for years now," the nun said. "He's a pro. I'll make sure he gets settled."

Patrick looked at his parents, then back at the beautiful young woman, who again had vanished. He kissed his mother's cheek, opting to wheel out of the lobby without a word to his father. Sister Margaret, Tito, and the pink lady followed down the long hospital hallway.

Mr. Flannery, conscious of the unexpected obvious slight, shouted toward Patrick. "This is going to be a good week," he said, optimistically. "I can feel it."

No one in the small group turned to acknowledge the encouragement. His parents slowly walked away. Mrs. Flannery took her husband's hand, their fingers entwined like teenage sweethearts, when they exited the hospital confines.

§§§§

The weary, ancient, elevator doors opened, but intermittently jerked downward before coming to rest three inches below the floor. "These things are possessed'" Sister Margaret said, atypically trembling. "They are breaking down faster than we can repair them. Everyone, please watch your step."

The waiting passengers nervously departed. Even those who planned on traveling to different floors opted for another cab. Patrick easily popped the unexpected step. Staring at him from the opposite lobby wall was the ever-present oil portrait of the City Archbishop, whose eyes seem to eerily follow hallway pedestrians regardless of the direction they traveled.

"Priscilla," the nun continued, nervously. "I need a hand with Tito. And will someone call maintenance again about the elevator?"

Priscilla, a young, striking, slender Hispanic nurse with a tiny beauty mark under her right eye, ran down the hallway, taking the fretting boy from Sister Margaret.

"Bring Tito to his room," the nun insisted. "He's tired. Perhaps he would like some chocolate ice cream."

"Quieres helado, Tito?" the nurse asked, wiggling his toes.

The child looked at the two women. "Si, Si," he answered, quivering as Priscilla cuddled, speaking to him happily.

Sister Margaret turned to the impersonal pink lady. "I'll take over from here, thank you," she ordered, not pleased with the middling and fiddling nature.

The pink lady seemed a bit taken back. "Sister, of course you know hospital regulations strictly state I am required to escort the patient to the supervising nurse for hand-delivering chart purposes," she replied, aggressively.

Sister Margaret took the chart from the woman with one hand, before sternly pushing her back into a recently arrived elevator, with the other. Sister Margaret simply smiled, waving good-bye, when the doors closed on the shocked, administrator.

"I've run this area for twenty-two years," she said, dutifully warning. "I have my own regulations."

Patrick wheeled alongside the nun, strolling down the expansive corridor, with the sterile polished floors, glistening even against the dull, ceiling-mounted domed lights. As they passed the many rooms, they appeared to be occupied by patients and visiting family members.

The rooms were different sizes and configurations. Some held three beds, while most had just two. There were also sporadic private rooms for people who Patrick perceived to be privileged. While wheeling, he peered into the confined shelters, catching views of weary doctors, pre-occupied nurses and technicians. Some patients appeared to be attached to IVs, while one had her bed encased in a clear plastic oxygen tent.

It made him reflect on past St. Jude roommates who were admitted for various conditions. Additionally, the roomies resided in diverse parts of the metro area, including the five boroughs, northern New Jersey, Long Island, Connecticut, and like him, upstate New York.

Patrick remembered Mario, his roommate four or five years ago – he could not recall exactly. The teenager was born and raised in the Bronx and suffered severe burns in an apartment fire at the age of twelve. Patrick wondered about Danny from Nanuet, who, on a dare, tried to jump in an open car of a slow moving freight train, only to slip and fall underneath. Danny-boy survived but lost his left leg and arm in the process. He recalled Julio, from Queens, who shared his hospital room the year before last. It was not until Patrick's subsequent visit that he discovered Julio had succumbed to the ravaging brain tumor.

These varied roommates seemed to come and go. They were intensely in his life for brief times, and then were gone like the first winter season snowflake hitting unsuspecting, still warm pavement.

Those strong human bonds, which quickly cemented within the hospital barriers, evaporated once discharged. Patrick doubted this year would be any different.

An elderly custodian, with pronounced spider web-like facial lines, courtesy of forty-two years of smoking two packs a day of unfiltered cigarettes, climbed down a step ladder to interrupt the nun with a question regarding a missing equipment invoice. Patrick recognized the prickly Puerto Rican janitor who constantly carried out loud conversations, even when sweeping or mopping the floors, unaided. He continued wheeling ahead, slowing down at the nurse's station, fifteen yards from his waiting room.

Residents, nurses and aides were professionally jostling in the tiny alcove, filling prescriptions, answering ringing phones, and writing endless notes in stacked charts. They seemed oblivious to Patrick's presence. His face brightened when he saw the profile of one particular nurse, though.

"Mary," he said, grinning until the nurse pivoted, diminishing any excitement.

"Excuse me?" she asked.

"Uh, sorry," he said, astonished after realizing he was mistaken.

"You've been here so often we should name this room after you," Sister Margaret insisted, after catching up. "I'll see you later."

She began to leave, but stopped. "We're all lighting candles and praying for you," the nun said, her voice almost cracking.

Expressionless, he looked at the nun as she made her way back to the waiting janitor who was fishing for the errant receipt.

§§§§

Using his wheelchair as a battering ram, Patrick opened the door to his room, though much harder than intended, startling the middle-aged couple standing next to the furthest bed. It immediately dawned on Patrick he may have entered the room at an inopportune moment. Patrick was unable to see the occupant, but able to vaguely hear him say.

"I'm dying, and I'm dying being here," the voice said. "I just want to go home."

The middle-aged man and woman eyed him with suspect, like one would when watching from a living room window, a dubious door-to-door traveling salesperson visiting gullible neighbors. Patrick sensed they were a family of means. This was clearly an understatement since the gentleman's attire included a white dinner jacket, thin bowtie, with matching colored pants and shoes. The woman, elegantly dressed, wore a light lavender evening gown, her hair wrapped in exquisite layered buns held together by a diamond-encrusted pin. Additional extravagant diamonds draped from her neck, ears lobes, wrists and gloveless left hand. A tenth grade English language power word came to mind; ostentatious. The woman instantly grabbed the curtain with the satin glove covered hand.

She looked at him, crossly. "Can you please give us a few minutes of privacy?" the woman requested, callously.

"Mom, try to be nice," the unseen patient's weak voice protested.

"Of course," she eventually submitted but still closed the curtain. "I'm sorry."

It was the first instance he recalled ever feeling not welcomed in this home-away-from-home. Patrick rolled to the empty bed situated closest to the door, throwing his duffle bag and guitar on the neatly creased, heavily starched ivory white sheets. Pushing himself to the metal headstand, he bent down searching for an unseen thing underneath. After manhandling the firm mattress, he lifted a corner section, locating an object tied around the metal frame: A dusty, faded blue, wide hospital ID Bracelet.

It read, "PATRICK GERARD FLANNERY PATIENT: #13365/1983," his bracelet from last year. He untied the piece of colored plastic, tossing it into the trash canister. Retreating, he decided to reacquaint himself with the rest of the pediatric floor.

Yes, he was apprehensive when being admitted, however, Patrick's fear dissipated as soon as he entered this sanctuary. Being that this was his tenth stay at St. Jude's and the fifth time assigned to what was referred to as the "young adult room" on the pediatric floor, there was something calming and familiar about this rectangular space, with its large windows situated directly across from each bed. The room possessed the same four twin bed frames on creaky casters with unforgiving, thin mattresses, located in the identical positions, as well as the same varied duck-in-the-pond paintings hanging on the same peeling gray walls.

Before completely out of earshot, he overheard the distant conversation continue between mother and son. "Your father and I think it best that you stay here for another round of chemo," she said.

"You just don't get it, Mom," responded the hidden, defeated voice.

§§§§

Patrick finished the annual tour after reaching the open-air deck at the opposite end of the floor, around the corner from the bank of four elevators. He often referred to this porch as "his" while caring little for the others piggy-backed above and below decks.

Becoming sentimental, he recollected being introduced to this hideout by Lori, a just-out-of-college nurse, during his first St. Jude's interment. The decks overlooked a café patio, surrounded on all sides by the hodgepodge of connected hospital buildings.

Directly across from "Patrick's Porch" and down seven floors, sat the hospital laundry unit. On many warm nights, he would sneak out onto the deck to eavesdrop on the Haitian-born workers, who complained or bragged daily about women, their sex lives or politics, while smoking hand-rolled, illicit cigarettes. He envied their conversations as well as knowing at the end of specific shifts, they could freely leave their workplace, though just temporarily.

To some, the word porch or deck was a misnomer. The space was barely six feet deep by ten feet wide, just big enough for Patrick to turn his wheelchair. But it still represented freedom to him whenever admitted – this was his treasure island.

Since portions of the hospital were in dire need of upgrades, the lack of central air was a sore point to many. Most windows had been sealed shut and equipped with loud, offensive-looking individual cooling conditioning units. This enclave was his remaining refuge, where Patrick could breathe fresh air anytime. Granted, referring to this oxygen as "fresh" was a stretch, but it was still not contained or recirculated hospital-scented O2.

However, this hospital stay happened to occur as the early phases of a long overdue, badly needed capital improvement program. Presently, the decks were undergoing structural fortifying. This renovation project explained why numerous bags of cement, massive piles of bricks and random equipment remained behind by errant day laborers, blocking Patrick's path to the porch's railings.

"Freeze," he heard a voice exclaim.

Initially alarmed, Patrick thought it was hospital security chasing him away, but that made little sense since they never had in the past. Twisting his body to look behind, he recognized a familiar face. It was Mary...Mary Arnold, his favorite nurse. Patrick calculated he knew the 30ish, high-energy, very cute woman since his first or second St. Jude's visit. He noted Mary's perpetual cheeriness made her appear more like a high school classmate than a veteran caregiver.

Patrick beamed without hesitation for the first time since arriving. "Mary," he said, as she hugged him tightly, allowing him to relax in their embrace. "I've been wondering where you were."

"Where's everyone else?" he continued asking, as he smelled the scent of her perfume. "Susan? Lori?"

Mary sat on an abandoned crud-layered wheelbarrow, oblivious to the debris and dirt. "Susan married a doctor in March and moved to Jersey, and Lori quit last month and headed out to California with every possession in a rented U-Haul," Mary stated, always the chinwag.

"They didn't wait for me," he teased. "I'm graduating from high school this year, you know."

"Sorry, good-looking," Mary countered. "That's still jailbait."

"But, you guys always watch the "soaps" with me at lunch," he protested, feeling nostalgic. "What are we going to do this year?"

"It means you're stuck with me in bed," Mary said, her tender backside finally aching, remembering she had originally snuck behind Patrick to return him to the room.

She was not certain if the pain was a result of aging or the rough surface. Nonetheless, she needed to stand. Not noticing the dirt stains on her white uniform, she did, however, note Patrick's physical changes. His voice was obviously deeper, the baby fat gone, his face now chiseled, appearing much taller, even while sitting in the wheelchair.

"And what's this with my deck," he wondered. "What's going on? This has always been my hangout."

"Not this year, babe," Mary said. "It's closed for repairs. The contractor always forgets to lock the door."

Mary had always been partial to Patrick. "Let's get you back to your bed and out of these street clothes," she whispered in his ear while leaning on the chair's push handles after turning the corner near the elevators, heading toward his room.

"You want to help?" he asked trying not to babble or turn red.

"Honey, I'd love to but I'm on duty."

"You say that every year," Patrick volunteered.

§§§§

Mary wheeled the pet patient into his room only to be called away to assist another nurse handling a transfusion emergency. Patrick noticed a tall, deceivingly lanky, deeply tanned kid with near-perfect hair, unpacking personal possessions on the next bed. The roommate appeared to be the same age, but seemed a bit out of place, wearing a burgundy silk bathrobe, charcoal silk pajamas, and velvet slippers. A thick, pirate-like, black patch covered his right eye. The only thing missing seemed to be a Cuban cigar.

Silently, Patrick pushed himself to his bed. The curtain to the bed furthest away was still partially closed. That roommate was now alone, but seemingly sleeping.

The intruder looked up at this wheelchair user while fastidiously placing other garments on his assigned bedding. He keenly inspected the mobility device like a seasoned car buyer. If first impressions mattered, Patrick guessed the roommate was simply curious.

"Hey," the kid said in a heavy, but friendly, New York City accent. "Welcome ta my room."

For whatever reason, Patrick felt compelled to act picayunish to this homesteader. "No, welcome to my room," he said.

If the kid was slighted by the retort, he did not show it. "Whateva," he replied, returning to smooth out the few remaining wrinkles on the laid-out clothes.

Patrick reached into his duffle bag, removing a warm Pepsi. Hearing the pop of the can opening, the roomie reached over to shake Patrick's hand.

"I'm Tony. Tony Telesco."

"Patrick Flannery," he said, as they let go of an extended handshake, both squeezing too hard.

He tossed a Pepsi at Tony who caught it, effortlessly. Patrick began the task at hand of settling into the usual cubed area. Grabbing the duffle bag, he turned it upside down, dumping the contents onto his bed. He was now done unpacking. Toothpaste, toothbrush, dental floss, shampoo, conditioner, comb, blow dryer, pajamas, comic books, cookies, chips, gum, soda, candy bars, Drake's cakes, Ring Dings, magazines, acne cream, deodorant, radio, books, and other oddities occupied the mattress surface.

Impressed by the stash, Tony sauntered over. "What do ya got, Ironside?" he asked. "Man, you don't pack light."

Patrick instantly determined his new roommate meant no disrespect, deciding to ignore the dated television series reference. Tony persistently sifted through the stuff on the bed like an elderly flea market professional at a weekend mom-and-pop garage sale – hoping to discover unsuspecting buried treasure. With a smirk, he held up the Hardy Boys book.

Patrick snatched the paperback away. "It was a gift from my mother," he adamantly protested. He tore the paperback up using his teeth, spitting the shredded pages to the floor.

"Yous welcome to any of my things," Tony said, watching, with amusement, as he opened up one of Patrick's bags of Peanut M & M's. He fluidly lofted one up in the air, opened his mouth, catching it on its gravitational downward path.

Patrick wanted to change out of his street clothes, but Tony was making little effort to give unspoken privacy, forcing him to undress in front of a guy he hardly knew.

Since he could remember, Patrick had been overly sensitive about his body, wondering how it was perceived by others, especially his legs, which had naturally atrophied some. In fact, he still had a difficult time seeing his reflection in a mirror while naked or topless.

The school district waived any and all physical education requirements, so he was not forced to participate in gym classes – he doubted any childhood friend had ever seen him wearing shorts, considering he only swam in St. Jude's pool. He found himself speculating, actually worrying more about what women would think when seeing his reedy lower extremities, the first time.

But he was already surprisingly comfortable with this new stranger. As he pondered their exchange, he was not certain if it was Tony he found trusting or their comfortable, familiar environment.

Again, from experience, he knew it was not atypical to quickly bond with his hospital mates.

"Thanks, T," he said, still dressing. "What's mine is yours, too. The food here sucks. I always bring enough supplies to last a couple of weeks."

"Hey, what happened to your eye?" Patrick continued, asking.

Tony had emptied the rest of the Peanut M&M's on his bed, neatly organizing the candies by colors, arranging them in formations as if they were opposing armies preparing for battle. Patrick cavalierly rolled up his street clothes, alarming the new roommate.

"Say, man, be careful wid ya clothes, man," he warned, indignantly. "Ya can't be throwin' dem around like dat. Wrinkles ain't in, ya know."

Patrick had slipped into his gray Puma T-shirt, before pulling up matching sweatpants. "So, what happened to your eye?" he repeated.

"Me and my boys got into it wid some spics in da neighbahood," Tony said, proudly, pulling up the black silk pajama top to display a prominent stomach wound. "We was kickin' ass when one of dem pulled a knife and got me here in my eye and my ribs, but missed my manhood area, if ya know what I mean."

"Where you from?" he followed-up.

"Brooklyn."

"Why are you in St. Jude's?" Patrick peppered away with questions, per usual. "Why not a Brooklyn hospital?"

"Hey, ya know what dey got in dere?" he asked emphatically.

"They got doctas," Tony profoundly went on, informing Patrick while checking himself in a handheld mirror. "Here at St. Jude's dey got artists. They say they's gonna make me handsomer than before – like dats possible."

"You in a gang?" he asked, even more curious about this new companion.

"Yous soundin' like a DA or somethin," Tony said, now mixing up all the M&M's into one large pile in the middle of his bed. "It's my gang."

Patrick already concluded that whatever Tony confessed was, for the most part, probably true. Yes, this Brooklyn kid was an obvious braggart, but he could sense the soul struggled to be basically honest.

Tony felt he needed to further establish his authenticity with Patrick. "One of my main boys will be visiting dis week," he said, incorrectly sensing skepticism. "By the way, where ya from?"

Patrick shoved his stuff into his nightstand. "Upstate New York," he answered. "Near West Point."

"You know, the military academy," he ventured, sounding helpful to Tony who seemed distracted by the remaining candy.

The West Point reference clearly did not register. "Oh yeahhhhhhh," he said, a bit puzzled, his mouth entirely full of crushed chocolate. "So what happened to ya? Why are ya in da chair?"

Patrick's face suddenly tightened. "Because I can't walk," he said, looking out one of the room's window.

"Oh," Tony responded, swallowing the last remnants of the sweets.

This at first made sense, but then he looked back, confused. "What da fuck?" he asked.

"Actually, I used to be able to walk, but I had the football accident," Patrick said, reminiscing. "You know, last year's state championship game in Buffalo. In fact, you probably read about it. It was in all the papers. I was All-State Quarterback."

The Brooklyn native gulped down most of the Pepsi, "Yeahhh," he malleably confirmed. "Yous was da guy?"

"Yep, that was me," he responded, cockily. "We were down by a field goal. Fourth quarter. Two seconds left on the clock and as I was scrambling to throw the ball down field, I was blind-sided by their nose tackle and hurt my spine. Didn't even see my receiver catch the Hail Mary pass. Ironically, we still won the game."

"Shit, I rememba."

"Whoa," he said naturally, after sliding from the wheelchair into his bed, causing both legs to unpredictably spasm, slamming him back onto the hard mattress.

His roommate jumped, frightened by the unorthodox jerking. "What da fuck," he exclaimed. "Ya ok?"

The spasms were no longer big deals to Patrick. Basically, they were common occurrences, apt to erupt when sitting in his wheelchair in a specific position for extended periods, providing his hips and knees the opportunity to tighten. "Just a spasm," he said. "It happens all the time."

"Geez, I'm sorry about the accident," Tony replied, apologetically.

"Nothing to be sorry about," Patrick said, without giving it a second thought.

Tony finished consuming the pop. After crushing the aluminum can with his hands, he tossed it into the shared wired wastebasket positioned between their beds.

He helped himself to another carbonated beverage. "Being paralyzed, though," he said. "How old are ya?"

"Seventeen," he replied. "I'm starting my senior year in high school."

"Me, too," Tony returned, as if they had something special in common. "I mean, ya know, I'm seventeen, but I voluntarily volunteered to repeat a couple of grades. Hey, ya paralyzed from the waist down, right. Can ya use ya thing, ya know. Can ya fuck?"

Fucking was a subject he knew little about and avoided, especially with a person who he recently crossed paths with. "I, uh, don't know," he said, honestly, fidgeting, looking around the room for a possible escape route.

"What da ya mean ya don't know? Can ya get a hard on? Tony choked, spilling some of the pop on his silk pajamas, jumping for a towel, seemingly inordinately protective of his attire.

Patrick nodded yes. He was having a difficult time figuring this new roommate out, having already revealed more to him than anyone else in the past. In some ways, that realization made him sad.

Tony thought about this sexual predicament. "How far have ya gone?" he asked, curiously, suddenly playing the role as sex therapist.

Still speaking, he walked over to the room sink to wash his hands, and more importantly, to ensure the immaculate mane was still properly in place. Before breaking his gape from the mirror, he tinkered with the black patch. Patrick, still apprehensive the direction this conversation was heading, had not replied.

"Come on," he bellowed. "Don't be 'barrassed. Ya can tell me. Come on! Ya ever get some tits? Some snatch?"

"Snatch?" he replied, puzzled.

Patrick was both trapped and cornered, allowing himself to be boxed in on this virginity subject. His remaining defense was to keep future responses to a minimum.

"Come on," he said. "Ya ever been to first base? Second?"

"I've, I've never even kissed a girl," he finally admitted.

"No shit," Tony said, wondering how someone could have deprived themselves of basic sexual necessities. "Why haven't ya 'den? Ya scared? Everybody is scared. A good-looking guy like ya can't be no virgin, ya know. And don't even give me no wheelchair bullshit! I heard dat if ya stay a virgin long enough, ya can become a homo. Dat's a verifiable fact."

A horrible look crossed the Italian's face. "Ya ain't a homo, are ya?" he asked.

The thought was nonsense, Patrick knew, but still he understood a line had to be drawn immediately to protect his sexual identity or it might prove to be a long week. Homosexuality was a word he had not given much thought to, to date. Of course, school jocks bullied classmates classified as nerds unmercifully for being sissies, fags, gay, homo, simply weaker or vulnerable. It was not until this very moment, did he realize the damage this label caused innocent victims who were just trying to survive in school.

Suddenly, his mind systemically pulled from brain files, the number of instances when he was with a group of popular kids who berated, for no reason except to transfer their insecurities. Perhaps he had rationalized that since he never actually lobbed the insults, he was not at fault. However, after now having to defend himself, he knew better. Not once did he come to a victim's defense, which in his heart-of-hearts, made him complicit. This newly identified character flaw necessitated reflection and address, but at this very moment, he needed to confront Tony.

"No," he said.

The Brooklynite seemed skeptical. "I don't know," he prodded, unimpressed. "You was readin' that 'Hard Boys' book."

Correcting him was already becoming wearisome. "First, it's 'The Hardy Boys,' he said. "Second, like I already stated, my mother bought the book. I mean, fuck no."

"I did it for da first time, ya know, when I was almost twelve with my sixteen year-old babysitter," he volunteered, now placated and climbing back in bed. "Wheelchair or no wheelchair, if ya hang wid me, ya gotta fuck. I gotta reputation, ya know. Capisce?"

Patrick was already exhausted from this conversation. Flipping on his radio, the 99X radio DJ, hawked for the ninety-ninth caller to phone in with the "Phrase That Pays" to win a station T-shirt, along with an album of the caller's choice.

"The heat wave is still on," the DJ, Harry Hurricane, proclaimed. "People on the beaches better head home 'cause ya all have to get up for work in the morning. Here's a little music for the long drive home."

§§§§

A young baseball player stood alone in the outfield, watching the action taking place at home plate. A fly ball was suddenly hit his way, requiring him to race in the direction of the spiraling object, but his legs would not move. The boy looked down to investigate, only to discover the limbs were missing. Off in the distance, a sweet, gentle voice softly called out a name.

§§§§

Mary entered the room dragging a blood pressure monitor, awakening him from the rerun dream – or was it a nightmare – he was not certain. She sat on the side of the bed; a constant stream of saliva ran from the side of his mouth onto the cement-hard pillow.

"Wake up, handsome," she said touching his forehead with a long, ringless index finger. "It's time to rise & shine."

Patrick's voice sounded hoarse. "Huh?" he responded groggily, momentarily incoherent, wiping the spittle from his chin with a nearby towel.

"It's me," she said, now running the slender finger along his nose, pestering. "Here, give me your arm."

"What time is it?" he asked, repositioning himself upright.

Mary stood, wanting to begin taking the readings with the awkward looking machine. "6:55, love," she said too merrily for this early hour. "It's time for morning vitals."

Patrick closed his eyes, trying to recapture last seconds of shut-eye, but Mary shoved an electric thermometer under his tongue while at the same time, pumping air into the rubber material quickly wrapped around his left bicep and tricep. He peeked at the thermometer, watching digital numbers fly upward, eventually beeping, to indicate a normal temperature.

"Father Burke will be here any minute with Communion," Mary informed him. "Then breakfast. You have a busy day today. We're going get you into the braces this afternoon."

The name of the priest jarred his memory. "Fr. Burke is still here?" Patrick asked.

"Well you might not recognize him," she replied, heading toward Tony's bed, repeating the daily morning routine. "Rumor is he has some sort of neurological condition. I'm not sure what, though. If you ask me, it doesn't look good. His hands are always shaking."

Mary smacked the Italian's feet, waking him. "Jesus Christ," Tony said, visibly aggravated. "Who da fuck is wakin' me..."

"If you curse one more time, Mr. T, I'll take your temperature from another body cavity," she warned, a little annoyed, cutting him off.

The veiled threat brought a smile to Patrick's face before he dozed off.

§§§§

60

A deep, raspy voice intruded on Patrick's semi-sleep zone, startling him, which in turn, frightened the ancient priest standing next to his bed holding a chalice full of wine and a plate of host offerings. Droplets of red wine found a new home on the bed's white sheets.

Father Burke looked thin, doddering, diminished, Patrick immediately thought. In fact, had Mary not mentioned the same hospital priest would be stopping by, he would never had recognized the once robust man, with artificially colored red hair, who befriended him during his initial indoctrination. They had now known each other for nearly a decade, and over that period, a special bond had been solidified. Patrick could tell this man loved his mission, swearing fealty to his God.

But the still booming voice compensated for the apparent frailty. "The Body of Christ," the priest commanded.

"Father, I must have fallen asleep," he said apologetically. "How are you?"

The priest responded, but more to himself. "Behind schedule," he said, apparently not recognizing Patrick. "Need to catch up."

Father Burke reached for a wafer, fumbling. Securing one, he leaned toward Patrick, a receiving tongue extended. Forgetting to provide an option for a sip of wine, the clergyman moved away, repeating the ritual with Tony. He left the roommates to complete the remaining morning Communion hospital rounds.

The roommates looked at each other. "Dat was a priest?" Tony asked, sullenly chuckling.

"Yeah, but he's usually a lot friendlier," he countered, trying to protect the old man's honor.

"I thought he'd be a lot more hospital workin' in a hospital."

"You mean hospitable," again correcting him.

"Whateva."

Patrick spied beyond Tony, noticing the curtain continued surrounding the far bed, hearing nothing except labored breathing. Turning on his radio, the 99X DJ, "Dancing Donnie," barked, updating listeners with a morning commute report.

"Don't look now but here's da chow," Tony said, nodding, as an orderly, who Patrick failed to identify, carried two breakfast trays. Wearing a skin hugging T-shirt and pants, he rested one tray on each bedstand.

A decorous voice announced the spoken words with a pretentious air. "Good morning, gentleman," the orderly said, exposing startlingly brindled colored teeth. "My name is Gregory. Do not complain about culinary choices or quality. I am not the chef, instead I am the designated medical official assigned with courier responsibilities."

Gregory hooked his thumbs into the holes on top of the light beige dish covers, and with theatrical embellishment, unveiled what constituted breakfast: A pint sized carton of milk, a half-filled hazy plastic cup of orange juice, two rock-hard fried egg, three mysterious meat strips, burnt toast, and a green banana.

"Bon appetit," he said, with precise inflection.

After Gregory left, the roommates peered blankly at the bland food collection. Tentatively, Tony placed a fork in the middle of one egg which remained upright upon release.

They both reached into Patrick's snack collection, pulling out pink colored Hostess cupcakes. "Dey get us up early for dis?" Tony pondered, over Dancing Donnie's voice again barking for the 99th caller with the "Phrase That Pays."

§§§§

Patrick opened one eye, squinting like an inebriated Popeye. Mary was back, but this time holding an empty syringe, rubber hose, and swabs. She poked his right arm in search of a viable vein. Fortunately, the years of upper body exercising created easy-to-locate pipeline sources.

"I vant your blood, handsome," she said in a spontaneous Countess Vampire imitation, stabbing his arm without seeking approval. "You know the routine for today: X-rays and physical therapy. But first it's time to bathe."

"Is the bath self-serve or drive thru?" he asked, suggestively.

Mary threw a water-saturated wash cloth at Patrick, hitting his youthful face. "That hurt?" she asked after finishing the blood removal and planting a Band-Aid on his wound.

Unsure if Mary meant the soggy fabric, or blood stealing, regardless, she did not wait for a response. "I need urine samples every hour," Mary instructed. "Let's rock-n-roll."

In the background "Dancing Donnie" cued Phil Collin's "Sussudio," then sought another 99th caller to phone in with the "Phrase That Pays."

Patrick's first, heavily scheduled day, raced by:

7:44 AM: Patrick's room – He bathed using a shallow basin, lathering whenever successfully grabbing the slippery, unsinkable bar of Ivory soap. Inadvertent water splashed, wetting his once dry bed sheets.

8:09 AM: Hallway bathroom – He urinated into a small plastic cup, easily filling it to the brim. Patrick handed the warmish container to an ill-at-ease, plain-looking student nurse.

8:31 AM: Patrick's room/bed – An Asian doctor wearing thick glasses, which constantly slid down his wide, short nose, checked Patrick's paralysis, jabbing him with an unusually large safety pin, beginning at his ankles and moving up. Initially, the jabs were timid, but became more aggressive with every stab. Ugly red dots appeared after each hard prick, causing him to yell "OUCH!" when finally feeling the pain.

8:55 AM: Patrick's room/bed – Mary drew blood from his right middle finger.

9:17 AM: The hallway bathroom – He passed a half-full plastic cup of urine to the same uncomfortable nursing student.

9:40 AM: The room/bed – The Asian doctor, his eyeglasses still needing constant adjusting, stood next to a single resident, jabbing Patrick, creating the additional discomfort.

10:09 AM: Hospital X-ray room – Patrick lying on a high metal table for numerous body X-rays.

10:55 AM: Patrick's room/bed – Mary again drew blood; this time from his right wrist.

11:12 AM: The hallway bathroom – Shrugging, he handed a one-quarter cup of urine to the nursing student.

11:24 AM: Patrick's room/bed – The Asian doctor with an expanding crowd of residents surrounded his bed. Some of the physicians appeared interested, while the rest merely stood nearby focusing more on their pagers. Exhausted from this act, the human pin cushion responded to the almost stabbing before the level of paralysis to avert expected pain. This "miracle" astounded the Asian doctor, requiring him to re-jab to re-establish their findings.

11:53 AM: Hospital X-ray room – More X-rays.

12:20 PM: Patrick's room/bed – Mary, who wanted additional blood, began prodding his left arm.

12:37 PM: Patrick's room/bed – Gregory served an odorless, brown substance covering a plate full of clumpy white rice. The roommates opted for a box of Ring Dings.

1:08 PM: Patrick's room/bed – Alone in his bed, watching *All My Children*, Tony again mocked his sexuality for being a soap opera fan.

1:19 PM: Patrick's room/bed – Patrick continued watching the daytime television drama. Mary, and a second attractive nurse, entered with their take-out salads, kissed his flushed cheeks before climbing in the twin bed. Tony, jaw dropping, scrambled for the remote, turning his TV to the same channel.

1:35 PM: Patrick's room/bed – The Asian doctor's non-stop jabbing caused Patrick to yell out in agony. However, this time, the physician had not yet poked, instead holding the glistening safety pin in the air.

2:08 PM: Patrick's room/bed – Now a crew of residents, and medical students encircled Patrick. The Doctor raised the infamous safety pin, but before attacking, the human guinea pig ordered them all out.

2:39 PM: Hospital therapy room – A middle-aged, sturdy black male physical therapist with a close-cropped receding hairline, assisted Patrick into a whirlpool.

3:08 PM: Hospital therapy room – The same PT did range of motions with Patrick's legs.

3:28 PM: Hospital therapy room – Patrick stood upright between parallel bars, Band-Aids covering both arms. The PT knelt, securely holding his waist. He strained walking down the narrow path, feeling feverish as sweat poured down his upper body, soaking the New York Mets T-shirt. Suddenly he began to falter, forcing the PT to guide him back into the ever-waiting wheelchair.

4:19 PM: Hallway bathroom – An exasperated Patrick handed the cup to the resigned student nurse. Meager drops of urine were in the cup this final time.

4:45 PM: Patrick's room/bed – Finally, Mary could not find a prominent vein on Patrick's spent, outstretched arms. In a defeatist posture, he offered his throat.

§§§§

At the end of the strenuous day, a drained Patrick waited for an elevator outside the PT ward occupied by a hunch-backed local senior citizen hospital volunteer, who appeared to have fallen asleep while leaning on the back of his chair's push handles. When one of the elevator doors finally opened, Patrick discovered the beautiful young woman from the hospital lobby inside, casually talking with a handsome doctor, who also used a sleek, sports wheelchair. She looked at Patrick with her ever-present radiant smile. Embarrassment got the best of him, though, forcing his gaze to the floor, but when looking back, an agitated and jealous Patrick discovered the elevator had continued toward its destination leaving him and the hospital volunteer behind.

§§§§

Patrick raced down the hall toward his room. Upon entering, he noted Tony was again in front of the sink mirror. For the first time, the curtain around the far bed was pulled back, exposing a skeleton-thin patient frantically dialing an outdated rotary phone, all room radios blasted in the background as if in stereo.

"No more calls, we have a winner," said Cricket T, the station's lone female disc jockey.

"Yuck foo," screamed the formerly hidden roommate, slamming down the receiver.

A body-bruised Patrick tentatively lifted himself out of the wheelchair, into his crisply made bed. The finally visible roommate, with shoulder-length, straight blond hair, but yellowish complexion, was connected to an IV.

"Ah Matt, come on," Tony commented, smiling.

"I want to win that contest," Matt protested, turning down the volume.

"Ya only win an album and T-shirt," he said. "Ya could buy 'em."

"But I want to win it…before it's too late," he responded.

Patrick munched on a single Oreo, listening to the exchange. Impressed with the final reflection results, Tony walked over to his bed to lie down, too.

"You must be Patrick," Matt said, looking over at the empty wheelchair, waving.

"And you Matt," he answered, returning the wave.

"Yeah, Matt Clark."

"Si," Patrick responded, using one of only a handful of words he remembered from Mrs. Llama's introductory 10th grade Spanish class. "How are you feeling?"

"I'm starved," Matt said. "Can I steal something from you? I'll be your best friend."

Looking into his open top dresser door, Patrick retrieved, and tossed over, a double-Twinkie package and Pepsi. Matt attempted an unsuccessful, single-handed catch with his non-IV hand, his slow, drug-induced reflexes just barely knocked the refreshments down from the air onto the mattress. Scooping-up the treats, he straightened, propping pillows behind his body, hoping to provide a more comfortable sitting position.

"Say, about the other day, sorry for my mom's rudeness," he said between savage chews, dispatching each Twinkie in two massive bites, relishing the chemically induced flavors. "She can be pretty direct at times."

The ravenous roommate failed to notice the white cream blanketing his mouth. "No big deal, man," Patrick said. "Are you from the City?"

"Yeah," he responded, his stomach feeling satisfied, between swallows of Pepsi. "I overheard last night you're from upstate."

"Near dat military academy, ya know, East Point," Tony confidently voiced in, also enjoying a cola.

"That's West Point," Matt interjected, laughing along with Patrick at the gaff.

"Dat's what I said," the Brooklyn boy protested, still ruminating his mistake.

Matt rubbed his stiff neck, obviously in discomfort. "This cancer is starting to make my muscles stiff," he confessed. "I need some TLC from a pretty young thing PT ASAP."

"PT?" Tony wondered aloud.

"Physical therapist," Patrick volunteered.

"Oh, I know what muscle ya got stiff, and yous don't need a PT for dat," he replied, trying to reestablish face.

Benny, a burly Jamaican with a braided beard and endless extended rows of long dreadlocks, entered, miraculously displaying four dinner trays, one for each bed. Grimacing, Tony inspected the offering only to discover mushy pasta, covered in watery marinara sauce, accompanied by one large impenetrable meatball, and a limp roll. The wilted salad swam in dressing, while a bright canned fruit cocktail was provided as dessert. Insulted, the authentic Italian dumped the main course into a nearby stainless steel bed pan, carrying it out of the room. The nurse walked over to Matt's bed, discretely pulling a brown paper bag from his waistband, handing the bag to Matt in exchange for a small wad of bills.

Patrick met Benny for the first time during last year's required hospital stay. He affectionately referred to the nurse as "Voo-Doo Mon" after catching him perform a mystical religious ceremony on the floor porch in the middle of the night. Patrick was certain there were no animal sacrifices, but he never received a precise answer from Benny what he was praying to and for what. But Voo-Doo Man established himself to be a caring worker, assisting patients any way he could, even if his methods were perceived as being somewhat unorthodox, even to his peers.

"Thanks," he said. "Hey, are my parents still bugging everyone for that private room?"

"Ain't gonna find no private room here this week, Mon," Benny said, simply. "We're sold out."

"My parents want to sequester my suffering," he said to Patrick, watching as the nurse left the room deep in conversation with no one in particular. "They're accustomed to getting what they want."

"Our roommate here is loaded," Tony said, blabbing, as if bestowing privileged and confidential information. "Ya shoudda seen da fuckin' rock his mudda wus wearin'."

"Cut me some slack, man," Matt protested, embarrassed by his family's tendency toward extravagance.

"Hey, I don't live on no Park Avenue," he countered, lifting a genuine crystal vase, overflowing with fresh exotic flowers from the windowsill next to Matt's bed stand.

Without warning, the fourth roommate limped in. He was a tall black teenager, with an outdated extended Afro, which Jimmy Hendrix probably paid handsomely for in the late '60s. He wore a hospital-issued robe, pajamas, and slippers. His heavily wrapped left leg forced him to walk with the use of used wooden crutches. Tony eyed the intruder suspiciously as the black roommate made his way to the remaining empty bed, eagerly devouring the waiting suspect spaghetti dinner.

"I'd like you to meet our new roommate," Matt announced. "His name is William T. Dubose, III. But he likes to be called Pearl."

Tony turned away and muttered. "Der goes da room," he said.

"Patrick Flannery," Patrick said, ignoring Tony while lifting himself from the bed. He wheeled over to shake hands between bites, noticing Pearl's extremely long fingers.

"Wassup?" Pearl replied in an unexpected deep voice.

"What happened to your leg?" he asked.

Pearl stroked the clean leg wrapping with his hands. "Fucked up my knee playin' ball," he said while inhaling dinner.

"Basketball?" Patrick guessed.

"No, African handball," Tony said, uninvited, still provoking. "Whaddya think a nig...dey play?"

"Fuck you, wop," Pearl exploded at the insult, spitting out food remnants.

"Listen, cool the racist shit while we're all sharing a room," Matt ordered, preaching tolerance. The two potential combatants, glared from opposite ends of the fortunately long room. However, neither made an aggressive first move.

Tony stared at Pearl for several more seconds, finally shrugging, walking away. "If I don't hear no wop words, he won't hear no nigga shit," he said, again muttering.

"Screw the black and white shit, guys," Matt continued. "Look at what Benny inappropriately smuggled in for me. Care to celebrate?"

He pulled out a large bottle of dark rum from the paper bag, and with a flourish, twisted off the bottle cap, relishing a long mouthful.

"Celebrate what?" Patrick asked.

"My next round of chemo doesn't start until tomorrow night," Matt said.

"I can't...I, I mean I don't drink," Patrick said, apologetically watching Tony immodestly swig.

Tony surprised Patrick by shoving the bottle in his mouth, forcing the contents down a non-expecting throat. Patrick's eyes rapidly widened as he gagged on the ingested alcohol.

"Ya do now," Tony said.

Just minutes ago the fighting Italian was ready to go toe-to-toe with Pearl, but the rum had already softened any edginess. He sifted through Patrick's bedstand drawer, in search of munchies. The boys ate

Yodels, and salty thin pretzel sticks, guzzling the passed around rum, laughing, as the tension in the room dissipated.

"What's with this chemo shit?" Pearl inquired.

"It sucks," Matt emphatically pointed out, before sucking down another gulp of rum.

"Ya know, I heard dem chemo drugs make ya balls fall off," Tony said.

"They didn't last time," Matt countered.

"Is the chemo working?" Patrick asked.

"It was," Matt said, pointedly.

"Should you really be drinking?" Patrick ventured.

"Like it matters anymore," Matt answered, quietly taking one last liberal swig from the bottle.

Benny reentered their space, almost trotting, this time carrying an immense panoply basket of fruit. The four ogled as he balanced it on Matt's bed.

"It's from your mother, Mon," he shouted over his shoulder, exiting the room again. "She probably wants to make sure you're eating healthy."

"Shit," Matt said aloud. "Look at that."

Pearl grabbed a grapefruit-sized navel orange from the basket, tossing it on the air like a basketball, catching it and spinning it on his index finger.

"You really do play," Patrick added, witnessing him shuffle around his back, like a genuine member of the Harlem Globetrotters.

"Whattaya think?" Tony asked. "He's black."

"I played a little JV ball," Matt said. "Maybe we could play a game of one-on-one sometime."

Pearl jumped off the remaining good leg, twisting and gyrating around. Taking a long distant shot, the orange cleanly landed in an open top pitcher full of water close to Tony's bed, making a loud plopping sound. He eyed a stunned Matt.

"Anytime," he responded candidly, before looking at Patrick. "Say, bro, why you riding 'round in that chair?"

"I was injured in the state swim meet last year," he said in his story-telling way. "Hurt myself on my final flip turn in the 100 meter freestyle. I was leading by two seconds. You probably read about it."

"Yeah," Pearl said, knowingly.

"I thought ya was hurt playing foot...," Tony wondered aloud, puzzled.

"Why they call you "Pearl?" Patrick asked, deflecting before the inebriated Tony could finish.

"No reason," Pearl said. "I always liked Pearls."

"This is the first time I've ever been drunk," the inexperienced fuzzy tongued Patrick slurred, attempting to touch his nose with his left pinky. "Am I drunk?"

"Jesus, he's a virgin, ya know, he's never had booze before," Tony said, half-kidding. "Next thing ya will tell me dat ya never seen a porno flick, ya know what I'm sayin'?"

Patrick looked away, attempting to not answer. "I give up," Tony conceded, throwing a pillow at him, the look revealing what he suspected. "I'm sure ya've never been on a motorcycle before either. So, ya know, when we get outta here, I'll take ya for a ride around my neighborhood, okay?"

"You've got a bike?" Patrick asked, tossing the pillow back.

Tony seemed almost insulted by the comment. "Bike?" he remarked, incredulously. "Fuck no. I gotta Harley."

"This is it," Matt said excitedly because the radio DJ asked for the ninety-ninth caller with the "Phrase That Pays."

Matt scrambled for his bedside phone, nearly knocking over the bottle of rum in the process. Tony lunged, catching it midair before hitting the floor. He lofted the bottle back to Patrick.

Matt's first call failed to get through. "Yuck foo," Matt screamed.

"Yuck foo?" Patrick asked.

"Fuck you backwards," Matt responded instinctively, dialing repeatedly.

Pearl limped over to Matt's bed, looking through the basket of fruit. "Ya mind?" Pearl asked, taking a ripe plum.

He glanced at Tony. "Want one?" Pearl asked, proudly polishing the squeezy ripe fruit against the scratchy robe.

"Nah," he said, shoving several pretzel sticks into his mouth. "Dat stuff is good for ya, ya know?"

The DJ announced, "We have a winner. No more calls."

Matt reacted, kicking the fruit basket off his bed, permitting the many contents to fly in various directions. A single, Macintosh apple rolled up against one of Patrick's wheels, giving him an idea.

"You guys ever play fruit ball before?" Patrick asked.

Pearl wiped away the plum juice from his chin. "Fruitball?" asking, surprised to not know all organized sports.

"No, never," Matt said.

"What da fuck, fruitball?" Tony added, in a typical blustery fashion. "Sounds faggie ta me."

"Shut up," Matt demanded.

Patrick rounded up as much of the produce that would fit on his lap, wheeling out of their room. "Grab the rest of the fruit and follow me," he said boastfully.

§§§§

The expansive red-bricked hospital patio was empty except for the numerous circular white patio tables with matching white chairs stacked on top. Patio lights beamed a greenish tinge in the twilight hour.

All four roommates raced around the space using individual wheelchairs. They smashed into the furniture, knocking over chairs, like bumper cars. Continually fetching additional pieces of fruit for ammunition purposes, they kiddingly threw grapes, cherries, berries, even bananas, with abandon at one another. Pearl stopped, turned away from the action and quickly peeled a tangerine.

Patrick was familiar with this gladiator-like experience. Three years ago he began playing wheelchair basketball with disabled Vietnam Vets, in a gymnasium located at a local VA facility. Nice guys, yes, but all in dire need of emotional therapy. Timid of these much older, physically imposing teammates, he became a gifted passing point guard only because the position required taking the ball up court, and passing off before being drawn into the bedlam taking place underneath the basket.

This fruit fight was action packed, fun, and frantic until Pearl swiveled in his chair, faced the fray and took aim, throwing the peeled tangerine with a tinge of vengeance at Tony. With impeccable accuracy, it smacked the big Italian above the right ear, splattering over his perfectly placed hair, creating a matted mess, thus turning the contest into a battle.

What seemed like an eternity actually took mere seconds, as a pissed-off Tony pivoted his borrowed four-wheeler, in order to identify the assailant, eventually squaring-off with a defiant, spunky Pearl. Acting as if the spontaneous revelry had officially ended, the Italian climbed out of his chair, revengefully, to initiate a volatile tussle.

But before the two could initiate the fisticuffs, Benny called at them from the tenth floor porch. "Get your hospital butts up here before I get my ass fired," the disturbed nurse yelled, after lighting a self-made cigarette.

§§§§

A still inebriated, nude Patrick finished his shower in the communal stall not far from the designated floor restrooms. Sitting on a wall-mounted fold-down bench, his wheelchair sitting nearby, he put the still running hand-held shower head back in its holder. Grabbing the wheelchair, he pulled it along the wet ceramic floor. Since the accident, he had performed this type of transfer thousands of times, but this instant, he simply erred. Patrick began lifting himself into it, but without warning, the chair began to roll away.

Attempting to steady both himself and wheelchair, the sudden miscalculation instantly sobered him. With his body air-borne, Patrick sensed imminent danger, realizing he had forgotten to activate the brakes.

"Goddamn you," he swore, truly angry. "Get back here."

With the wheelchair refusing to fully cooperate, he continued suspending himself. The back-and-forth rocking denied him the needed leverage to get safely back onto the shower bench or to reach the brake mechanisms.

"You son of a bitch," he said, his temper worsening.

Patrick spied the stainless steel, wall-mounted shower grab bars. As the wheelchair continued straying, he lunged for one, but missed. Before crashing, he inadvertently knocked loose the still running handheld shower head, causing the device to flip about like an active electrical power wire. Landing on the slick floor with a loud thud, he futilely attempted subduing the shower head, clutching the chair.

His water slicked buttocks began sliding on the equally wet, smooth tiles. "Chair, I'm fucking gonna kill you."

Patrick's legs violently spasmed, flipping him backwards. Hitting his head against the hard wall, the handheld shower somehow lodged itself in the wheelchair, shooting a constant, high-pressured steady flow of hot water directly at his face.

Choking, he groped blindly for the chair. "Get the hell back here," he said, insanely.

Finding the wheelchair, he pulled it toward him a bit too hard, flipping it, and causing it to fall on top of him. Patrick punched and attacked his chair like an opponent in a televised catfight match.

"Help, somebody," he yelled, wildly. "Help me. I can't get up."

The shower door abruptly opened. The stunned pink lady stood at the entrance with an empty push cart, gawking at the unclothed Patrick pounding his wheelchair.

"Will you please help me?" he pleaded, recognizing, but not caring how pathetic he must have looked. "I can't get this fucking thing off."

"You're not wearing anything," she said, frozen in place.

Before she could respond, Benny swooped into the shower area after hearing the commotion. He turned off the hot, pulsing water, lifted the wheelchair upright, and threw an expansive cotton towel over Patrick, helping him off the floor and into the chair.

"Excuse me," Benny protested to the pink lady, clearly annoyed, closing the shower door to comfort and shield Patrick. "I got you, brother."

"I hate this fucking chair, Voo-Doo Man" a despondent Patrick said, tears running down his damp face. "I hate it. Hate it. Hate it…"

§§§§

Father Burke awakened him with a predictable jolt. Patrick's head pounded, his mouth tasting like metallic sand, as the priest leaned over, spilling the remaining Communion offerings on the sheets. The bewildered man frantically recovered the wafers with evident shaking hands.

§§§§

Well after sunup, Patrick opened his eyes, discovering Dr. Goodman sitting at the edge of the bed. His pulverized head felt like pizza dough before being tossed into a brick oven. Even the whirring of the outdated window-mounted air conditioner pained him. Tony's muffled snores echoed from beneath a blanket covering his head, only enhancing the cranium throbbing, making Patrick feel worse.

"Doctor," he muttered.

Patrick frequently thought his physician was an archetype for Marcus Welby, the good-natured family physician and lead character of a popular childhood TV show. The benign, brilliant medicine man was in his late '60s, with snowy white hair, a heavily creased face, but still quite spry and adventurous. Elderly, yes, but no one ever questioned his acuity of mind.

The doctor was missing his thumb and index finger on his left writing hand, the result of a bomb defusing accident in Germany at the tail end of World War II. The injury prevented him from fulfilling his parent's dream of becoming a heart surgeon. Instead, he returned to the States, recovered from the physical loss after extensive therapy, and graduated from Harvard Medical School. Goodman focused his energies on orthopedics, settling in New York City and becoming a world-renown specialist in the fledging new field of rehabilitation medicine.

Dr. Goodman had been treating Patrick since his accident. A distant relative, who had worked many years for a famous Hollywood starlet, used the movie star's influence to connect Patrick's parents with the highly respected physician. Although Goodman had a heart of gold, with retirement nearing, he had become more and more selective with the strenuous case load. But he was immediately drawn to Patrick's spirit and drive when meeting the youngster as a courtesy consult after the child boldly announced to everyone within earshot that, wheelchair or no wheelchair, one day he was going to be President of the United States. Without further thought or debate, Goodman agreed to take him on as a patient, working with the family in their quest to have Patrick walk again.

"Get up," Goodman said, clearly peeved. "I brought some food so we could spend a little quiet time together. But you know the rules. All my young patients kiss me on the cheek hello and good-bye."

Patrick smiled at the annual command from the wise man, who had a breakfast from the outside world waiting at his bed stand. Gingerly, he sat up, kissing the physician's cheek, an expression of obeisance, as expected. Looking around the untidy room with empty soda cans and food wrappers scattered about the floor, counters, and bedstands, Goodman pointed to an empty bottle of rum sitting on the wheelchair seat.

"You don't look well," the doctor said, sternly.

Patrick's head swirled. "I don't feel so well," he responded, his voice shaky, concerned he had violated a non-published hospital decorum. "I, I swear it was my first time."

"You should not be feeling so well," Dr. Goodman chided, upset of the breach of trust and privilege, pouring Patrick a glass of water from a nearby pitcher with a naval orange floating inside.

He handed the young patient the cup, as well as the three aspirins appearing in his non-injured hand like a magic card or coin trick. Patrick consumed the clear, non-alcoholic liquid with loud, flowing swallows.

He took the empty glass from him. "Here, eat this bagel, slowly," Dr. Goodman ordered.

While Patrick rubbed his exploding forehead, Dr. Goodman pulled a couple of fresh, just out-of-the-oven smelling, sesame bagels loaded with cream cheese, and two bottles of cranberry juice from the bag, meticulously placing everything next to Patrick.

"Listen, I don't approve of you drinking," Dr. Goodman said, officially putting Patrick on notice, but trying to minimize the controversy. "Don't you remember how you ended up in this chair?"

Feeling worthless, Patrick nibbled on the oversized baked wheat, spilling sesame seeds between his legs, sipping the cold, but refreshing juice. Already his mouth was losing the vile taste, and the aspirin slowly conquered the bongo playing in his head.

Dr. Goodman picked up the empty bottle of rum, placing it in his long, white medical jacket front pocket. "How did things go yesterday?" he asked, resting in Patrick's wheelchair.

As he forced some of the bagel down into his stomach, Patrick recalled his mother not tolerating her children talking with their mouths full. She had quite a few manner-related rules...all which were strictly enforced...like, no chewing with your mouth open, no elbows on the table, no shoes on the table, no combs or brushes on the table. The young patient was distracted by the sudden revelation that she had far too many table dictums.

"How did things go yesterday?" he repeated, louder.

Patrick snapped back to reality. "Oh, I had the X-rays and started PT," he said. "I wasn't able to walk with the braces. I tried, but I just couldn't do it."

Tony suddenly stirred, then erupted. Without warning, he threw his blanket off the bed, swiveled over the mattress's edge, tentatively touching his feet on the cold vinyl floor, his hair seeing better days.

The hungover Tony moaned, blindly heading for the room's sink. Spotting his reflection from the mounted mirror above the lavatory, only increased the grunting decibels. Tony twisted the faucet, putting his mouth underneath the flowing liquid.

"Fuck," he bellowed.

Tony inadvertently turned the incorrect knob, releasing hot water. He instantly corrected this error, but not fast enough to prevent minor scalding, letting the cool liquid parch his dry, and now tender, lips and tongue.

Dr. Goodman and Patrick watched the unpretentious performance from their prime house seats. Tony finished with the drink, leaving the room, failing to shut off the water and without acknowledging their presence.

Chuckling, the doctor got up from the bed, walked over to the sink to finish Tony's uncompleted environmental responsibilities. "I was told you had problems again with the braces," Dr. Goodman said, sitting back in the wheelchair.

"Honestly, that worries me," he continued, wanting to discuss the merits of his approach. "Your father tells me you've worked hard all year to build up the upper body and you do look like you've filled out quite a bit."

"The braces still too heavy?" Goodman inquired.

"Yes," he replied, concurring with a heavy, methodical nod. "It was like my legs were welded to the floor."

Dr. Goodman finished the bagel, wiping both hands and mouth before throwing the crumpled napkin into the brown bag. "Perhaps today we should first try you wearing the braces in the pool," he said, deviating from his original plan. "They'll feel lighter."

"Okay," Patrick responded, willing to try just about anything at this point.

"If that works, we'll do it again outside of water," Dr. Goodman continued, prudently.

"I just want out of this stupid chair," Patrick declared.

"Understood," the doctor said. "We all do. Let's see what happens."

Patrick played with his remaining bagel, hesitating. Dr. Goodman moved to leave, but sensed the boy had more to discuss or share.

"Is there something else?"

"Dr. Goodman, uh, I need to talk, I mean," said Patrick having a difficult time completing the sentence.

"What?"

Taking a deep breath, he finally found the courage to reveal the troubling thoughts. "About growing up," he said, feeling foolish. "I need to speak with you about growing up."

Puzzled, Dr. Goodman looked at him.

"I need to talk with you about, about...I need to know more about my body," he finally blurted. "I don't know anyone to talk to about sex."

Dr. Goodman studied Patrick, when a slight smile appeared. "Oh my, I'm getting old," he said, sounding apologetic. "Someone should have discussed these issues with you long ago. I can't help but think you're still a little boy."

"It's just that I can't talk with my parents about this," Patrick confessed. "They wouldn't understand."

Angry with himself, Dr. Goodman packed what remained of their breakfast into their makeshift trash bag, unintentionally getting cream cheese on his impaired hand. "Patrick, I have this new resident in my department," he volunteered, licking the spread remnants off his palm. "His name is Dr. Brennen. I think he would be a better sounding board on this topic. I'll make sure you two get together this afternoon."

He pulled back the curtain. "There's also a young PT intern working for me now," he informed him.

"So, you're not upset?" Patrick said, a bit facetiously.

"About misbehaving and drinking, I am," Dr. Goodman let him know. "About growing up? You should be annoyed with me. Now finish the bagel."

He started to leave, carrying his juice and refuse. "By the way, we will be doing tests on your bladder tomorrow," Dr. Goodman said, updating. "I'll be there. But I may be late. It's another busy visit for you."

Grumbling, Tony re-entered the room, shuffling to his bed, only to fall face-first onto the rock-hard pillow. Dr. Goodman, watching with amusement, looked one last time at Patrick, chortling to no one.

§§§§

Patrick entered the hospital PT swimming pool, immediately overcome by the familiar powerful chlorine odor. Coughing, partially choking on the smell, he surveyed the large underground aquatic room. At fifty meters long, six lanes wide, although not Olympic size, this was one of the largest indoor pools in Manhattan. The shallow end was barely three feet deep, with the opposite end designed and constructed with a depth to accommodate occasional community diving competitions. Lap lanes were set up daily after work hours when the hospital, for community-relation purposes, allowed neighbors to access the pool.

He was a prolific swimmer. In fact, it was incorporated into his daily physical therapy years ago. He was not a swimming phenom, but it beat the weight-lifting and other strength-building exercises advocated by his physical therapists and father.

Patrick found it interesting he was not a gifted swimmer before his accident. In fact, he was not much of one at all. At the age of five, he attended his first summer day camp. Patrick was required, as were all other campers, to be tested for swim-level class purposes. Having splashed his way barely 4-5 feet, put him in the "minnow" level just above the lowest ranked "tadpole" group.

But learning to swim was important to his mother, who was deathly afraid of water, having never recovered from a near drowning as a child at Rockaway Beach. Patrick read the yellow-brown, torn newspaper articles about the heroic college student who rescued her from a strong riptide on his very first day working as a lifeguard. But it was her fear that made it a requirement for Patrick and Dana to overcome any aquatic fears.

Dana enjoyed swimming so much, she became an active member of the town's youth swimming team, "The Sharks," achieving state-wide ranking in both freestyle and backstroke categories. Her passion for swimming grew in high school and, after successfully making the varsity team her freshman and sophomore years, she was expected to break most school records this season.

Patrick's swimming ability increased following the accident. Typically, he would park his wheelchair next to the diving board, slide his rump out to the end, to dive into the water from a seated position. Breast was his preferred stroke; it was the most convenient without the use of legs. And usually he would do sixty laps, which converted to three miles, per session.

Nothing seemed to have changed since swimming in the pool last year. In the deep end, the portable sling for patients who required assistance in the water remained firmly mounted to the floor. The only detected change worth noting, the hospital emblem, was now painted on the pool's floor, dead center. Directly across the water was Derrick, his assigned PT the previous four years, with a stopwatch in hand. Two other PTs, with their backs to him, guided a heavy-looking woman through the deep area.

Derrick, wearing a tad too-tight red racing Speedo, sat in a slick-wheelchair similar to Patrick's, but with severely cambered rear wheels, timing someone who furiously, yet gracefully, swam laps. Patrick rolled down the side of the pool, his legs extended to accommodate the heavy metal braces already locked around his lower body. The PT lifted himself from the chair, when the mysterious aqua-man finished, slapping the pool wall with an outstretched arm.

"You gotta shave three seconds off that time, man," Derrick commanded. "You're getting slower as you're getting older."

"C'mon man, I think it's your reflexes that are getting slow," the swimmer debated. "Maybe you need a new stopwatch."

Derrick pointed to his crotch. "I got your new stopwatch right here, buddy," he laughed at the young swimmer who Patrick spotted yesterday in the elevator with the stunning woman.

Patrick inadvertently interrupted their conversation. "What's up, Derrick?" he asked.

"Need a hand, P-man?" Derrick responded not looking up, still eying the timed finish.

"You're insulting me," Patrick said, reminding him. "I have it down to a science."

"Well, then get the science moving," he retorted, taking a phony impatient tone.

Patrick locked his wheelchair next to a pool ladder a few feet from the partially submerged parallel bars. Using the ladder, he tentatively lifted, placing his backside on the pool's edge. Derrick stood up and walked away. The finished swimmer recovered, and checked Patrick out.

"How's the water?" Patrick asked.

"It's nice."

Plopping-off the edge into freezing water, he surfaced with a loud scream. "Shit," he yelled, the echoed profanity heard by everyone.

Patrick faced him, holding onto the steel ladder. "I'd be freezing my balls off if I could feel them," he exclaimed. "I thought you said the water was nice?"

"Nice?" he retorted, innocently, while hoisting himself out of the pool, resting on the pool's edge. "No, I said, it's like ice."

For years, the hospital struggled with the water temperature controls, apparently possessed like the elevators. Countless respected city engineers could neither repair nor explain why some days the water was as warm as a hot tub, or on others, as chilly as the ocean the foolish Polar Bears annually frolicked in on New Year's Day. Some claimed the fluctuating temperature was simply "God's Will."

Patrick furiously treaded the clear, chemically treated water with one hand, trying to quickly warm-up. Catching his breath, the swimmer lifted his body and in one fluid motion moved from the edge into the wheelchair Derrick had been using. When safely in the chair, he looked back at the teenager, who continued adjusting to the frigid water.

"So you're Patrick?"

Patrick pumped his head "yes."

"I'm Dr. Brennen, but call me Brian," he volunteered and offered, rolling closer to the water. "I work with Dr. Goodman."

Patrick became a bit defensive. "You here to check me out?" he suggested.

"No," Brian said amused. "I'm doing laps on my break."

"Why?"

"Just keeping in shape," Brian pointed out. "Anyway, Goodman told me about you."

"What'd he say?" he responded, curious.

A distant female voice called out. "Stop loafing," the unidentified woman yelled. Surprised, Patrick whirled his head, glimpsing a beautiful woman standing on the diving board, pointing at him.

"I'm talking to you, Mark Spitz," she teased Patrick.

The stunning woman from the hospital lobby and elevator was now addressing him. Patrick began connecting the dots. It had to be the intern his doctor mentioned. She looked to be about twenty, petite, with perfectly shaped and sized breasts, curly dirty blond hair, that famous radiant winning smile, wearing a damp white polo shirt with the green St. Jude's seal. It was evident a black one-piece bathing suit tightly covered her athletic body underneath.

"You shouldn't be talking when you should be walking," she added.

Derrick slipped into the pool during this playful exchange, slogging up behind Patrick, gently guiding him in the water toward the parallel bars. After reaching the bars, Patrick steadied himself between them.

"Got it?" Derrick wondered.

"Got it," he stated, confidently.

The beautiful woman, still wearing her shirt, dove into the pool, swimming the entire length toward them like a porpoise underwater, resurfacing next to Derrick.

"So, Mr. Flannery, I understand we're going to have you walk in and not on water today," she remarked in a straightforward fashion.

"My dad will settle for me walking anywhere," Patrick said.

"What?" she asked, taking off her now drenched polo shirt, hurling it at Brian, who ducked in the nick of time.

"I've never tried this before," Patrick noted, as Derrick swam to assist the lone PT, struggling with the obese woman who dangled on the pool sling.

The young PT looked at Patrick. "That surprises me," she said, innocently, holding his elbows from behind.

"I saw you in the hospital lobby a couple of days ago," he mentioned. "What's your name?"

"I'm Edie," she said. "Edie Miller."

"Hi," he replied, words suddenly failing.

She grinned at the evident flustering. "You okay?" she asked, readying him between the bars.

"I'm fine," Patrick replied.

Letting go, Edie sallied back to help the now overmatched Derrick and PT comrade with getting the heavy-set woman safely out of the pool. Patrick, standing upright, watched her depart and caught as she snuck a brief look at her new patient.

"I bet the water got warmer," said Brian, sitting less than ten feet away in his own wheelchair.

Surprised and embarrassed, Patrick blushed. "You jerk off?" Brian casually wondered.

"Ex...excuse me?" Patrick said appalled, spitting out some chorine water.

"Relax," Brian said reassuringly. "Do you masturbate?"

"Uh, no, never, uh...well, okay, once," Patrick confessed reluctantly. "But, but it was, was an accident."

"Let me guess? You went directly to church?"

"Yeah, of course," Patrick said, smiling, sensing Brian was not being impertinent, having probably been in his shoes. "Who told you?"

"Walk," Edie yelled from a distance, more caring than nagging. It was unclear to Patrick if the three PTs were ever going to return the patient to her waiting massive chair.

"So, can you get a hard-on?" Brian asked, simply, but peppering, while he attempted to take a step.

Patrick moved one leg, but only inches. Though not totally relaxed with Brian, he was grateful for the chance to finally broach this once taboo subject.

"Uh, sure," he said after a few seconds. "I'm just not sure if I, I can perform, like my buddies."

Fruitlessly, Patrick exerted himself to move his other leg. Edie, Derrick, and the third PT continued skirmishing with their charge, her extreme weight causing the sling to precariously sway back and forth, midair.

He could not help but stare at Edie. "She is amazing," Brian said, reading his mind.

Although seeming futile, Patrick knew he needed to concentrate on the task at hand. "I can hardly move my legs in the water," he said, discouraged, grabbing the parallel bars as tightly as possible.

"Don't worry," the young doctor said reassuringly. "Just keep trying, man."

"If I can't walk in a pool, how can I expect to walk out of one?" he asked anxiously, jerking his upper body to the right and left hoping the momentum would aid in the successful moving of his body.

"Relax," the resident said. "Don't be so hard on yourself. Let's just feel the water for now.

"Do you use braces?" he asked.

He stopped for a moment, looking down at his submerged legs in the clear water. Patrick could feel the strength draining from his arms, the weight of the braces already affecting him.

"I tried, but they did not work for me," Brian said bluntly.

"I don't want to talk about it anymore," he returned, sighing. "Let's go back to erections."

"Erections?" Brian laughed loudly, purposely teasing.

Patrick cringed and glanced toward Edie, who he unexpectedly again caught looking his way. "Yeah," Patrick said, half-whispering.

"You heard about pump implants?"

"What?" he responded.

"The pump is like taking your blood pressure," Brian said, miming an inflating motion with his hands. "They surgically implant one down there, and you manually pump it up whenever needed."

"No," Patrick said. "C'mon. Really?"

"Seriously," the doctor said. "Granted, it can ruin a mood, if you catch my drift. Not your speed, huh?"

"Ah, no," he said emphatically.

"You know about the wonder drug?" Brian asked. "Papaverin?"

He shook his head no. This verbal exchange was also giving Patrick the benefit to catch a breath and regain some strength – he could feel his arms recharging.

"It's like a tranquilizer," explained the physician, almost cheerfully. "It lets the penis relax, thus no spasms, thus no blood loss, thus no loss of erection. In fact, it has a reverse affect. Because the penis is so relaxed it allows more blood to flow into the shaft, enhancing the erection."

"It's a pill?" he asked, not persuaded.

"No."

"A gel?" Patrick asked, now skeptical, but yearning to know more.

"Not even close," Brian said, pausing before elaborating. "You inject the drug into your penis."

Patrick turned white, but not because of anything related to the braces. "You have to stick a, a needle?" he asked, the news astounding him.

"Hey, it's no worse than what a diabetic goes through," Brain said, pausing. "Except for the injection location, of course."

"But, hey, most of us paras don't have complete feeling down there anyway," the older wheelchair user went on. "So you can inject the stuff without getting the full feeling of the needle, but you get maximum benefit from the result. Women will be calling you tripod."

"Do you do it?" Patrick asked, grimacing at the thought of a needle in that location.

"Hell, yes," Brian said, enthusiastically. "Two-hour erections are too hard to pass up."

"Two hours?" he countered, clearly impressed.

"Two hours."

"Where can I get some?" he wondered, as he let go of one of the parallel bars.

"Come on," Brian said, turning his chair in search of his ever-missing gym bag. "I'm a doctor."

Patrick smashed his fist into the water, too hard, because he felt himself slowly losing balance like an object being pushed too close to a table's edge. Brian located the gym bag sitting on a nearby bench and began loading his gear. At the other end of the pool Edie and Derrick had finally secured the woman safely into her chair. Everyone failed to see him teetering.

Frightened, and without enough time to yell out, Patrick plopped face first, like falling timber into the water, he banged his nose against a bar, splitting the flesh open.

Dazed and disoriented, he still instantly comprehended the present quandary. He was in trouble, but he discerned holding his breath was essential, however, oozing blood from the nose clouded any vision. Like an anchor, the weight of the braces quickly pulled Patrick to the pool floor, forcing him to jettison the braces from his body, but because he could not reach the release switches, it was impossible. His lungs began to ache as much as the injured nose.

By chance, the heavy woman, comfortably sitting in her wheelchair, wrapped in an enormous beach towel, was shocked at the sight of diluted blood quickly spreading in the water, forming a red cloud.

"Oh my," the weighty woman finally cried out.

Brian, hearing the scream, pivoted back to the water. "Jesus," he exclaimed.

Without thinking, the physician instinctively launched his chair into the pool causing them to separate – like Patrick's leg braces, the chair sank to the bottom, as Brian swam to Patrick.

Edie and Derrick turned, too, not grasping that Patrick was under water, in trouble, or that Brian was already in fast pursuit. Edie almost trampled the heavy woman when diving back into the pool.

Brian reached him but realized the combined weight of the boy and braces was simply too much to handle. Resurfacing, he quaffed in fresh air only to dive again to the besieged patient. This time he decided to lighten Patrick's load by removing the braces.

Patrick felt his chest was moments away from bursting, not certain how much longer he could last without fresh air. Turning, he could see bodies swimming toward him. Strangely, he was not frightened or alarmed with the life-threatening predicament. In a surreal moment, he somehow concluded drowning was not going to be his passing.

Derrick caught up to Edie, reaching Patrick concurrently as Brian managed releasing the last brace-locking mechanisms. They each grabbed an arm as the metals were unfastened from his body, freeing him to the surface. Brian assisted as best he could in securing their charge out of the water. After lifting him safely from the pool, Derrick retrieved Brian's wheelchair, which sat patiently next to the newly added hospital floor emblem.

Lying on the edge, Patrick continued coughing and spitting up water, gasping for air, which never tasted so good. His nose bled profusely, but overall he appeared unharmed. Edie grabbed a white hand towel, pressed it against the open wound, soaking and clotting the blood. Brian sat on the edge, prepared to offer needed medical assistance. Patrick came to, noticing her so tantalizing close to his face.

"Two hours sounds pretty good," he said wearily.

"What?" she asked, a peculiar look on her face.

Brian, relieved, he put his mouth to Patrick's ear whispering. "It is," he said.

Edie overheard the spoken cryptic words, looking at them both, curiously.

§§§§

Patrick wheeled from a smallish examination room, the remnants of the nose wound properly bandaged. Brian had been waiting in the cluttered far office reading outdated editions of "Boy's Life," "Catholic Weekly" and various catalogues spread over a chipped, light brown wooden coffee table. While the teenager was being treated, the resident took the opportunity to change into jeans and a button-down, blue striped oxford shirt, covered by a short white hospital coat.

"You look like you lost the fight," Brian quipped.

"How's the other guy?" Patrick replied.

Wheeling side-by-side down a wide, empty, nearly dark hospital corridor, they picked up their conversation where it left off an hour ago.

"And how about, like, a double dose?" Patrick peppered.

"Not recommended," Brian said. "The two-hour limit is precisely that – a limit. Too much and you take undesirable risks. I heard of a guy in Denver who shot himself up with 18 hours' worth."

"18 hours."

"Yeah, he had a great time, I guess," he volunteered. "The woman, or women, that is. But once it came down, it was down for good."

They reached the bank of elevators. Tired and ready to go home, Brian pushed the down arrow button while Patrick, needing to return to his above located room, pushed the other.

"He can't ever?"

The doctor acted like a basketball referee ejecting a player from a game after receipt of a second technical foul. "The man is forever out," he said, cautioning.

Derrick unexpectedly appeared behind the two wheelchairs, putting his hands on Patrick's push handles. "Men," Derrick said, not meaning to intrude.

"Hey, how about having children?" Patrick asked.

Derrick jumped in. "Sorry, I got three already."

"You never answered my ejaculation question before I almost drowned," Brian asked, the untimely reminder wiping the grin from everyone's face.

"I don't think so," Patrick answered. "I never have."

"With today's technology, we can artificially stimulate the ejaculation, refrigerate the sperm and inseminate your wife, girlfriend or whomever at a later date," said the doctor, trying to ease any worries. "When you're ready to make a deposit in our unique bank, we'll have you open an account."

"Cool," the veteran PT interjected.

"Come by before you check out so I can give you a sample and a prescription for more," Brian instructed while entering a recently arrived elevator.

"Great," Patrick said, profoundly grateful for Brian's kindness.

"Papaverin, right?" Derrick asked, as the door closed.

"Yeah."

"Cool."

§§§§

Derrick and Patrick waited alone for the elevator. One noisily arrived, but rested four feet above the floor. They looked at each other while the PT articulated their similar sentiments.

"We'll take the next one," he declared, as the doors to the malfunctioning silo departed, haunting, growling noises echoing from the shaft.

Derrick attempted to change the subject. "Brian's a good guy."

Patrick kept his eyes on the doors, but still responded. "Yeah, he seems cool," he concluded, inspired. "Now all I need is, is some girl. Someone who won't mind."

But he did not finish the thought, instead, subconsciously gesturing to his chair, patting his legs, finally running both hands along the rear wheels, Patrick's mood depressed by the reality. The next elevator arrived without incident, allowing them to both enter, tentatively.

§§§§

Although safely contained in the vertical car, indescribable noises thundered from above and below. They carefully watched the floor indicator lights as they worked their way upward.

"Ever think a woman who won't want you because of the chair ain't worth having?" Derrick finally volunteered.

Patrick looked up, but before answering, they reached his floor. He started to wheel to his home-away-from-home, however, the PT's firm grip on his chair indicated their destination plans had changed.

"What?" Patrick announced. "This is where my room is, Derrick."

"I know."

The PT smacked the top button, but before they continued on their way, Patrick looked out, noticing his father outside throwing Tito up into the air. The young child screamed with laughter as he defied and succumbed to gravity with every toss. Priscilla stood nearby, holding an oversized stuffed panda bear. His father spotted Patrick after catching the child, stopping, he held the excited boy in his arm. Jack Flannery trotted over to the elevator, and with his free hand, prevented the elevator from leaving.

"Dad?" he asked, in a surly tone. "What are you doing here?"

"Well, I stopped by to give Tito a present," Jack Flannery said, only partially true, while trying to adjust the squirming boy in his arms. "I…I also heard things did not go well with the braces. I wanted to tell you not to quit."

"Would you stop using the word quit," Patrick tersely protested, hitting the lit button again.

His father backed away while Priscilla, sensing an approaching family squall, took an uncooperative Tito from Jack.

"Come, Tito," she whispered, causing the young boy to squall. "Vente."

"You, you, you know, I'm giving it the best I can," Patrick said, exasperated, forgetting that Derrick still stood nearby. "I love you, Dad, but you have to leave me alone. You have to back off."

"Well, I, I mean…I can see your point, but," Jack Flannery replied, flustered.

The son cut the father off before he could finish. "See ya, Dad," he said, too curtly.

Patrick's father could only stare at his son, the two coming precariously close to the other's breaking point, making Derrick uncomfortable. A buzzing ordered the doors to press harder for closure. During the interruption, Jack attempted to regain his composure.

"Who do you think you are?" Jack Flannery demanded, galled at the attitude. "I didn't drive to the city to be treated like this by my teenage son."

"First, I didn't ask you to come, Dad," he said, testily. "Second, I don't want you here. Third, go home."

Patrick let go of the door, catching his father off guard. The obnoxious buzzing noise ceased when the doors abruptly shut. Mr. Flannery lost his remaining composure and began to yell, his words fading as the lift continued upward.

"Open this door now," Jack Flannery screamed, clearly antagonized. "Where do you think you're going?"

§§§§

The roof maintenance door opened with a loud bang, enabling Derrick to pull the wheelchair up the last step. After the slightly winded PT released the chair, Patrick regained control of his movements. Turning to look around, a bit reticent and in awe, his jaw quickly dropped at the breath-taking twilight setting.

Far away, Edie sat on comforter laid out on the roof surface. Although some sections were tarred, most of the exposed space was covered by 2x4 pieces of wood. Since Patrick left the pool, she had changed from her bathing suit into a loose, white linen blouse, tan shorts, and orange flip-flops.

Edie barely noticed their arrival, as she continued pulling endless cartons of Chinese food from two large, straining shopping bags. A moist mist hung in the air on this warm evening. As he approached, he noticed his guitar was resting on the old, scruffy purple quilt. Behind Edie, sundown city colors surrounded the roof's horizon like they did during shows at Patrick's high school's planetarium, the openness allowing Manhattan sounds to reach this temporary, secluded picnic area.

"When you need a hand getting down, you know, call me," Derrick announced. "I'm workin' late tonight."

Edie blew him a kiss as he saluted a good-bye and withdrew through the same maintenance door. Patrick wheeled around the roof space, checked out the view, then pointed to his guitar, near where she stood.

"I went to your room," she explained, answering his unspoken question. "It was empty, so I just grabbed it. I had no idea what kind of Chinese food you liked. I ordered a little bit of everything. Alright?"

"You kidding?" he replied, astonished.

§§§§

Looking disturbed, Jack Flannery stepped away from the elevator, leaning his body against the opposite wall. Within seconds, another cab opened, permitting a disheveled Dr. Goodman to exit. Immersed in reading a particularly large medical file, he clutched several more against his chest. Although preoccupied in thought, the physician stopped after passing Jack Flannery, sensing a familiar presence.

"Jack?" he asked, looking back. "Jack Flannery?"

Patrick's father was caught off guard, too. "Dr. Goodman," he said. "Hello."

The physician stepped aside, allowing other hospital personnel passage. "Please, please how many times do I have to ask you to call me Sam," he declared, as they both moved toward a nearby inviting couch with its right arm shabby because of old age. They sat, leaving the mid-section between them open.

"Sam," said Jack, embarrassingly. "What a nice surprise."

"What are you doing here?" Goodman asked, clearly concerned, picking at strands of fabric from the ancient sofa. "You look out of it. Is everything alright?"

Jack ran both hands through his thick hair, just wanting to leave the hospital and return home. "I saw my son," he said, sighing. "If I'm not mistaken, he told me to get lost."

"Well, forgetting he's still a teenager, there's much pressure this week," the doctor responded, knowing whatever verbal assault transpired, was not treasonous.

He looked at their longtime doctor. "How are things going?" Jack inquired, suddenly impatient and depressed. "How is my son doing?"

Goodman placed the medical files on the unoccupied cushion. "Honestly, not well," he confided. "He does not seem to be progressing with the braces."

"But we worked so hard this year," the dejected father said, looking as if hit by a freight train.

"It's not always about hard work," the doctor attempted to explain in order to relieve him of the evident distress. "Your boy is trying. That much I know."

"He is?"

"I can't buy you a beer at the hospital, but how about having a nightcap with me?" Dr. Goodman offered as countless patients and staff alike, walked by. It was the end of the day, he suddenly felt tired beyond his years, and he knew the setting should change for this conversation to continue. "I keep a bottle of single malt in my office for favorite friends."

"You know Patrick's accident was my fault," Jack Flannery said aloud to Dr. Goodman, the two exhausted men rose, entering the waiting crowded, elevator, which had arrived at an opportune time.

§§§§

Edie finished lighting the fifth and final candle strategically placed around the comforter, shedding ample light and flickering shadows. Her face gleamed off the reflecting light.

"You can use chopsticks, no?" she asked, pointing to the sublime dinner.

Patrick transferred out of the wheelchair, sitting across from Edie on the lumpy cloth. "No," he answered sheepishly, thinking he had always considered mastering them as trivial and not worth the effort.

She immediately gave him a condensed "chopstick for dummies" lesson, their hands occasionally touching. The innocent physical contact completely distracted him from comprehending any of her foreign utensil instructions. A gentle, warm, breeze played with her hair. Giving up on the stained wooden sticks, Patrick picked up his guitar and began playing "Don't Let The Green Grass Fool You."

After strumming the song from rote, Edie took the instrument from him, picking at the strings, amateurishly. "Nice Wilson Pickett tune," she commented.

"You know Wilson Pickett?"

"Get real," Edie said. "I know serious classic Soul."

"Yeah, right," he said, almost daring.

"You don't believe me?" she asked, shocked by the audacity.

"All right, cocky," she pushed on, wringing her hands in anticipation of their contest. "Up for a challenge? Test me. You name the song, I'll name the singer."

Thus began a quickly organized, rapid fire Q & A game.

"You Know The Reason Why," Patrick began.

"The Ebonys," she responded without hesitating.

"When The World's At Peace," he countered.

"The O'Jays," Edie replied, too quickly for his liking.

"Love Train."

"Bunny Sigler," said the PT, nonchalantly with amazing accuracy.

"When Will I See You Again," Patrick said, nervousness creeping into his voice.

Edie clapped noticing his bravado was wavering. "The Three Degrees," she laughed, relishing in her success.

He looked up to the sky as if only God could give him the one song that would stump his unexpected, worthy opponent.

"Me & Mrs. Jones."

"Easy," she answered breezily. "Billy Paul."

Patrick stammered. "Um, "Ooh Child," he grasped.

Edie began rapidly slapping her thighs, sensing victory was around the corner. "Which version?" she challenged. "The Fifth Staircase or Dee Dee Sharp?"

Patrick realized he had backed himself into a corner with no escape. "Dee Dee Sharp?" he asked.

"Gotcha," she shouted. "I win."

The PT celebrated by waving her arms in triumph, causing Patrick to smile as he watched her rub it in. After pinching his arms, hard, she eventually calmed down to refocus her attention on the waiting Chinese food, softly singing "Ooh Child" out loud.

"Been coming to St. Jude's for years, and I've never accessed the roof before," he volunteered, looking around the city skyline. "Feel like I'm at the Jersey Shore."

"The best are summer nights on the beach," she added, while Patrick began drumming the food containers using his neglected chopsticks.

"It's completely dark," Edie continued, wistfully. "You can't see the waves except for the caps, but you sit there listening to them as the wind whips against your face."

Patrick persisted fiddling with the eating devices, but slowed down, eventually stopping, astonished by the wonderment in her reminiscent words

Her memories transported Edie to a different time...High school to be exact. Raised near Princeton, NJ, Edie spent summers on Long Beach Island, or LBI – the only child of somewhat vacant, emotionally removed parents. Her father was an accountant, but would have probably preferred a life as a filmmaker. To compensate for his lack of confidence to pursue his true calling, he traveled everywhere with a bulky video camera, purchased second-hand from a Philadelphia television affiliate, taping family celebrations, car accidents, people shopping at supermarkets, in hopes of one day editing an undecided personal masterpiece.

Her mother was the daughter of the Cantor at the local Synagogue in Margate, just outside Atlantic City. Her dream was to study acting, and make her mark on Broadway. Instead, she dutifully listened to religiously observant parents, studying to be a school teacher. A safe occupation, they claimed, one providing a pension, which they lacked in their approaching retirement. And for the last thirty years that's what she did five days a week, ten months a year – taught fifth grade at Fostertown Elementary School in East Brunswick.

Edie's parents met at the Paramount movie theater in Montclair while watching West Side Story for different reasons – he for the art of films, she for the art of acting. Their paths crossing was a fluke they later demised, and the subsequent marriage a mistake. Their lives ended up being comprised of compromises…including their union.

The marriage produced a lone daughter who sensed the undercurrent of unhappiness between parents from an early age. Although she swore her life would be different, Edie began suspecting that perhaps it was, in fact, too similar already.

The inadvertent canny investment her father made shortly after her birth was the purchase of their Jersey Shore summer home. Had it not been for an intoxicated local banker bragging too loudly in the bar of a private golf club, Edie's dad would never had known about the opportunity. The founding partner of Mr. Miller's midsize accounting firm, Tom Carlino, annually invited him for a round of golf and then dinner, including several pre and post cocktails. Mr. Miller wondered if the parsimonious employer considered the outing part of the company's employment compensation package.

While Carlino was relieving himself after consuming three Old Fashions, Mr. Miller sat alone at the table, nursing his one and only Manhattan, listening to the various conversations at nearby stools. The drunken banker's dialogue caught and subsequently reeled in his undivided attention. He boasted to fellow smashed golfing partners about an inside foreclosure taking place the following afternoon, which would net him a stunning getaway Beach Haven home for an unheard of price of $75,000. He crowed about quadrupling his money in mere weeks simply by flipping the investment.

The next day, Mr. Miller, scrambled together every miscellaneous rainy day savings, submitting a bid, exceeding the banker's by $500, thus securing a majestic two-family, six bedroom house overlooking the island's bay.

Summers were Edie's refuge from the daily drab existence in the Miller household. It allowed her to spend the entire July and August months working as both a life guard and waitress.

Typically, her mother stayed with her on the upper level while the lower floor was rented out to relatives or family friends who lacked the financial resources to own their own getaways, but could afford one or two week rentals. Mr. Miller rarely joined his family on weekends, preferring the solitude their departure provided in Princeton.

Edie shuddered at her bipolar memories. "Wearing your favorite old sweatshirt, you sit on an even older ragged blanket," she said. "Drinking cheap red wine out of a paper cup, or better yet, right out of the bottle. It's like complete romance, even if you're alone. You spend the entire night there until the sun rises in the distant horizon."

She stopped playing with a cold sesame noodle.

"I, I feel terrible about, about this af...," Edie said, fidgeting, when Patrick picked at some fried rice with a plastic fork.

"What do you have to feel ter...," he tried cutting her off.

"I should have been wi...," Edie said talking over Patrick.

"It wasn't your fault."

"But in my capacity...," she said, uncomfortably.

They both stopped, looking at each other, cracking up.

"Seriously, I'm finishing my physical therapy internship this week," she volunteered after taking a spoonful of hot & sour soup. "I've been interning here for six months. You drowning would have put a damper on my evaluation. Of course, I'd lie and say it was an aberration"

Edie, still simpering, changed the subject. "How's the food?" she inquired. "Try some of the General's Chicken."

"It's different, but good," he volunteered. "To be honest, this is a novelty because I've never tried Chinese food before."

"Seriously?" she exclaimed, almost spitting out food forcing her to quickly wipe her mouth with a tiny, thin white paper napkin. "Never? C'mon. I was practically nursed on this stuff."

Using her chopsticks, she expertly sampled a large fried dumpling straight from the grease-stained box. Patrick reached into one of the food bags pulling out another fresh napkin for his dinner companion.

"Hey, I'm an Irish Catholic," Patrick said, defensively. "My mom's idea of an exotic meal is pizza with Canadian bacon on it."

He handed her the clean napkin as Edie gave another one of her infectious smiles. "Canadian bacon is exotic?" she asked.

"Listen, the Irish are big on basics," Patrick attempted to explain, naturally. "There are potatoes, corn beef and cabbage. And beer, can't forget the beer."

Edie doubled over. She crumpled up her napkin, winging it, just missing his head. Feeling comfortable, he leaned closer to her.

"Let me share something with you," she said, with authority. "Whenever you enter a New York City Chinese restaurant at peak times on Saturday nights, count the number of Jewish people eating and kibitzing. If at least half of the customers are Jews, you know the place is good. We have an affinity for this stuff."

"You're Jewish?" Patrick asked, the surprise in his voice evident.

"Miller doesn't sound Jewish enough for you?" Edie teased, but continued. "That tidbit I just shared. Well, my grandfather repeated it every time we went out to our neighborhood Chinese restaurant. He would tell it like you never heard this story before. And we ate at that place every Saturday. My granddad drove the rest of us crazy."

Edie instinctively began to play with her gold engagement ring, a cumbersome diamond anchoring the center of the band. Patrick had failed to notice the ring until now. Leaning away from her, his moment of optimism vanished. Not that he was stunned — in retrospect, it never dawned on him that Edie might have a boyfriend or even worse, a fiancé.

Patrick paused before responding. "I just saw my father at the elevator," he said, neglecting his food.

"What?" she replied, sounding genuine. "Is everything okay?"

"He drives me crazy," Patrick said. "We kinda had a fight."

"About what?" Edie asked, her concern growing.

"The braces."

"Regardless how old we are, our parents will always be our parents," Edie disclosed. "They never stop worrying about their offspring."

"I, I just feel," Patrick said, not being able to articulate the proper words to adequately finish his thought.

"You feel bad?" she observed, completing his sentence. "Well, guilt is one thing Irish Catholics and Jews have in common."

She picked up and broke opened a fortune cookie, looked at the sliver of paper with the written message, smiling to herself. "It's blank," she said out loud.

Patrick was not paying attention, instead his anger festered. "I've got enough pressure from everyone about walking again," he said, almost to himself. "I don't want him around, and I don't need him reminding me this is my last chance."

Edie passed a cookie, attempting to calm him down. "Don't worry so much about it," she counseled. "He's probably just as afraid as you are."

"About what?"

"About you spending the rest of your life using a wheelchair," she tried to explain. "I mean, you're his son."

"A son who uses a wheelchair," Patrick responded, dejected.

"Sounds like you need to cut him some slack," Edie suggested.

He looked up at a nearby skyscraper, knowing he agreed with her sentiment. Although Patrick's heart wanted to change the subject, stubbornness overruled his instincts.

"If it doesn't happen this week, then, uh, uh," he said, again struggling to finish his thought. "Look at what happened today. Nothing. I'm going to let my dad down, let everyone down."

"You can't worry about everyone else," she responded, reassuringly. "You've worked hard for you, not for them. I'm sure your dad will understand. But will you?"

Seconds passed between them before words were again uttered. She put the top back on the open soup container.

"You think I'm afraid to spend the rest of my life using a wheelchair?" he asked, the looming question finally uttered.

"I don't know," Edie answered, but then followed up with the million dollar question. "Are you?"

Patrick looked away, pulling at his wheelchair for no apparent reason. "Yes," he said. "It has frightened me virtually every day since the accident."

"There's nothing wrong with being afraid," she tried to counsel. "We're all afraid of something."

Patrick decided to turn the table on his eating companion. "Yeah, what are you scared of?" he asked.

Edie looked at her oily-laden plate, then back at him. "We're talking about you," she replied, it was the best she could do for an answer.

"Come on," Patrick boldly pushed, curiosity getting the better of him. "I'm telling you some deep stuff here."

Edie stood, walked over to the roof's edge, watching a silent heat lightning storm erupt on the Jersey side of the Hudson River. She was not certain if the sky light show was a precursor for a more violent storm. Edie bent her upper body over the waist-high brick barrier, peering down 7th Avenue trying to hear a young couple bicker about nothing, as the pulsating siren of an approaching ambulance grew louder.

She made an instant decision to be forthcoming. "Well," she began to reveal, admitting her shortcomings. "I'm supposed to be getting married next summer. But already I have doubts."

Patrick had to shout over the blaring siren. "Aren't you too young to get married?" he asked.

"Tell me about it," she said.

"We met when I was a freshman in high school," Edie continued, walking back to rest in his wheelchair, absently picking at the guitar strings. "He was a senior. Todd is the only guy I've dated. In fact, he's the only person I've ever slept or had sex with."

"I guess it's all relative," he said. "I mean, speaking as a virgin, you're still one up on me."

"I'm only 22," Edie confessed, thinking about her reliable fiancé. "I was 19 when we did it for the first time."

Startled by her impulsive intimacy, he listened without resentment, his face flushed, though. "I'm petrified of doing it for the first time," he blurted.

"So was I, silly." she said. Now her inflection was coy.

The affectionate use of "silly" caused him to redden. "But you didn't have to worry about a physical impairment getting in the way," Patrick confessed, plagued by guilt and not wanting to be a burden. "I'm so afraid I'll let down my first woman. A part of me thinks I should lose my virginity to a hooker to see what I can and can't do. But then that Irish-Catholic guilt kicks in again."

"Are you hoping for special dispensation from the Pope?" Edie inquired, smiling.

"I'm serious," Patrick said, while she laughed, putting down the guitar to sit directly next to him on the comforter.

"Your first time should be with a special friend," she offered. "Someone who cares about you and who you care about. You also should both be attracted to each other."

They both looked away, silence engulfing their comfort zone. She gazed upward, searching for visible stars in the sky, however impossible because of the city glow.

"Edie, what would you do differently if you could relive high school and college?"

She answered with initial silence. Incredibly, the City became silent, too. She took her attention away from the sky, and instead looked into his eyes, contemplating an idea or thought.

"Not get so serious so quickly," Edie finally answered, maybe a bit too openly. "Meet more good-looking guys like you. But what am I saying, you're statutory."

"But not in New Hampshire," Patrick said, jokingly. "I read somewhere the age of consent is fourteen."

Edie giggled again, snatching his not opened cookie. "Read your fortune," she said, with a tinge of flirtation. "Then I need to get you back downstairs before Sister Margaret calls the cops on me."

With that, Edie jumped up, closing the strewn food containers, wondering how two people could have made such a mess so quickly. She placed the leftovers in the shopping bags while Patrick lifted himself back into his chair. As they folded the comforter together, distant cars honking their horns radiated in the City below.

§§§§

The garage doors were opened on the warm summer evening. As the bright florescent lights illuminated the space with an artificial glow, at the far end of the driveway, fireflies flickered against the night sky.

A subdued Jack Flannery sat alone on the bench press table, his legs spread wide with a cardboard box sitting opened between them. Other identical boxes were scattered around the otherwise barren floor. An old baseball glove, charcoal baseball cap, even a small, still unclean matching colored jersey were spread around him.

He was as exhausted as he looked, with a rare five o'clock shadow covering his cheeks, chin, and lower lip – absentmindedly scratching the stubble. Jack had not changed clothes, however, the disheveled blue blazer rested across his lap.

He was unsure of how long he had been sitting in the garage, in solitude. He drove directly home after sharing a straight-up Scotch with Sam, initially thinking the road trip home would enable him to make sense of the many troubles preoccupying his mind. But instead, the quiet ride only provided the opportunity to drill deeper into his worries, thus intensifying raw emotions.

For the first time in many years he thought about his childhood pangs. Unfortunately, he could not recall his father, Gene, who died from a massive heart attack when Jack was just 14 months old. He had two older sisters, who possessed demons and goals similar to his own; get as far away, as quickly as possible, from their crazed, alcoholic mother.

His mom, for unexplained reasons, raised her three children in abject poverty. This fact, although not a happy story, took a perverse angle following her death – falling down the long front steps of the church's elementary school in a drunken stupor, after attending the weekly Wednesday evening Bingo outing. Shortly after her burial, Jack was contacted by an unknown attorney, with news his mother's estate had assets in excess of $1.5 million dollars, to be equally split among the three children.

At the reading of his mother's will, Jack discovered his penny-pinching mother had actually been an astute investor in blue chip stocks beginning shortly after the stock collapse of '29.

Although this inheritance secured college tuitions for Patrick and Dana, as well as paying off the few family debts and their mortgage, he never came to terms with the inheritance justifying the many times he left the dinner table, as a child, still hungry or having difficulty falling asleep on cold winter nights because his mother refused to pay basic utility bills.

It was not until entering Rice, his Catholic high school, did he realize how poor his family appeared to be. If not for his imposing physical presence and pugilistic prowess, Jack would surely have been hazed by classmates for being the only student wearing a hand-me-down school blazer from a distant cousin, with sleeves so short, they exposed the entire shirt cuffs. Most of his clothes were from the same relative. Their apartment was sparsely furnished, and cupboards typically barren.

His mother also possessed this incessant sick desire to emotionally pit child-against-child. During his senior year, Jack escaped for a long weekend to the Catskills only to be pounced on by a starving cat upon returning because she failed to feed the animal in his absence. By the time of this incident, his older sisters had fled the apartment, married, and were raising young families in surrounding New York suburbs, leaving him alone to handle his provider's unstable state of mind.

This particular instance, Jack made the mistake and compounded the problem by asking her why she had neglected to provide food for the pet. This door opening permitted his mother to slander his siblings, claiming they had ignored requests to assist in buying food in her feeble condition. Sadly, his mother was inherently a cruel, angry individual who continually tried to cast her foreboding shadow over the very ones she was charged to nourish.

Without an elaborate plan for the future, and weary of living amid chaos, Jack enlisted in the military the day after graduation, thinking it would provide an opportunity to experience the world. And it did just that by stationing him in France, Germany, California and Korea during the four-year enlistment. Following the honorable discharge, Jack tested and was selected to be a New York State Trooper. He was now six months from his twenty-first year on the force.

He met his future wife at a childhood friend's wedding, the day after he completed Trooper boot camp. She refused to remove her prized, full-length black cashmere jacket from an empty chair at the lower Eastside bar where post-reception celebrations had migrated. They began dating, became engaged and married within eighteen months. Patrick entered their world shortly before their third wedding anniversary.

At the outset, Jack's rudimentary goal was to offer stability for their children. Admittedly this terrified him since he had little guidance or templates to work from. Eventually, the adopted mantra was to do the exact opposite of his neglectful mother. He wished to work hard, provide for them financially, and to be a positive presence and influence in their lives. Not over-the-top prosperous, they were secure even with the required financial sacrifices Patrick's rehabilitation required.

Initially, everything was proceeding as planned until that eventful Saturday evening in August. Although Jack assumed he had a fairly constructive relationship with Patrick, there was an evident disconnection the day his eldest child became a paraplegic. This severing seemed to widen during passing years.

But clearly, today was not a good one. Jack did not anticipate a confrontation and was evidently ill prepared for Patrick's verbal assault. Visibly hurt and feeling ashamed, he wondered what he was doing wrong as a father. That aspect rattled his core. It frightened Jack that perhaps he had become tyrannical with his only son.

Tapping both feet to a non-existent song, he held a framed picture, the glass smudged with fingerprints. Mrs. Flannery walked into the hot, sticky open-air area clutching two sweating bottles of beer. At first he failed to notice her company, until a reflection appeared on the picture crystal.

She immediately knew he had been looking at the same Little League team picture her spouse was often engrossed with whenever forlorn. Mrs. Flannery placed the glistening bottles on the gray cement floor, silently picking up items, efficiently placing them back into their respected boxes. Once complete, she gently pulled the photo from Jack's grasp, though he continued staring ahead.

Mrs. Flannery placed it with the other dusty mementos, kicking the single containers closer to the side walls. She returned to her spouse, tucking one of the bottles of brew into his open hands. Always protective, she dearly wanted to resurrect his deflated spirits. Instead, she took a short sip, straddled him from behind, gently rubbing his stiff, aching shoulders, hoping to rid the current possessed pessimism.

Nursing their drinks, they continued sitting together on the bench press that unseasonably hot summer evening, watching a silent, white, full moon.

§§§§

The door to the hospital room was unexpectedly closed when he returned with Edie. Generally, the nurses or Sister Margaret wanted them kept opened until lights were ordered off. Because everyone in the room was nearing eighteen, the directive was usually enforced around 10:30 PM to deter any potential shenanigans.

When they entered, Pearl and Tony had invaded Patrick's bed. Pearl was lying on his back adroitly spinning a worn Nerf ball from his middle finger while Tony sat in one of the unforgiving metallic visitor chairs, feet propped on the bed, absorbing an unfolded centerfold in an ancient Playboy magazine. The sight of Edie caused Pearl to lose control of the ball and Tony to chuck the thick magazine under the bedstand.

"Men, meet Edie," he said, noticing Matt's shut curtain, a radio playing a bit too loudly from behind. "She's a PT intern."

"Hello, guys," she said, cheerfully.

Tony and Pearl could only ogle. For once, the Brooklynite was speechless. Edie casually walked over, stopping just inches away, slowly bent down to scoop up the exposed risqué centerfold from the floor. After placing it on Tony's lap, she made a retreat. Tony muttered a garbled appreciation, distracting Edie long enough for Pearl to ease himself off the bed, backing away from the uninvited visitor, as if frightened of catching a cold.

Edie had a sudden idea to spice up the surprising scenario. "See you tomorrow for our next session, handsome," she said to Patrick, her inflection filled with sexual innuendo.

She touched the bandage, speckled with Manhattan pollution specks. "You were great tonight," she purred. "Oh, and I'm sorry about the rough stuff."

Edie softly kissed his forehead, winking as she disappeared down the hallway. A few seconds passed before Tony and Pearl could compose themselves.

"It was my first time tonight, guys," Patrick announced, proudly.

"No," Tony screamed, jumping out of his chair, the soft porn magazine falling to the floor. "No fuckin' way."

Pearl pointed to the nostril appendages. "Was she really rough?" he asked.

Patrick surmised the roommate had taken the unintentional bait. Tony picked up the Nerf ball from the bed, squeezing it, strutting around their room.

"Yo, Stallion," Patrick called out, appreciating the jocularity. "I was talking about dinner. I had Chinese food for the first time."

Tony froze, looking around the room for unreciprocated moral support. He pouted, heaving the Nerf at Patrick before doing a solid back bed dive, rattling the metal frame.

"Pearl, ya believe dis guy?" he said sourly. "He tried to pull my chain, ya know. Just for dat, ya might not get to meet Gina tonight."

Patrick wheeled up to the empty bed, did a swift transfer, tossing the round sponge back and forth with Pearl. "Gina?" he asked, perplexed. "Who's Gina?"

Tony sat up in his bed flashing a shit-eating grin knowing the tables, or hand, had suddenly turned.

"His boy was here," Pearl said, pointing at a gloating Tony, the enunciation indicated some evidence of tension. "Not lucky for us he's coming back in a few minutes. But he left a little gift that Matt's still inspecting."

Patrick's roommates both nodded toward the closed curtains. Although the radio continued blasting, he precipitously became aware of other sounds from the far away bed. Patrick could only imagine who Tony's friend was and what he was like. Regardless, he sensed trouble was brewing, like an approaching migraine taking hold in one's brain.

"If ya apologize nicely, maybe I'll let ya borrow her for a while," Tony said.

Abruptly, Matt's curtain opened with a flourish. Wearing only boxers, he was upright with a mammoth unlit Cuban protruding from his mouth. An object darted by on the other side of Matt's bed. At first glance, Patrick was not certain what he saw, but then deduced it was a person, a young woman in fact, with tightly permed hair and thick facial make-up, in disarray. As the mystery woman applied fresh lipstick with one hand, she straightened a light lavender T-shirt, cut just below small, but perky breasts with the other.

"Gina, dis is the otha guy I as tellin' ya about," he said, winking at him. "Patrick, dis is Gina. She's my old babysitter. Rememba?"

"Nice ta meet cha," she said, speaking with a New York City accent which incredibly, was heavier than Tony's, causing Patrick to struggle understanding her words.

"Tonn, where's da bafroom? I gotta rinse."

Patrick looked at Matt, his smiling, half-naked roommate wallowing in bed chomping the unlit stogie, but then refocused on Gina, actually, more on her pants, when she rounded the bed. They were a bright white, and appeared spray painted on her not-an-ounce-of-fat, glowing, bronzed body. He wondered how she could breathe or move when wearing them.

"It's at the end of the hallway," Matt volunteered.

They silently watched her leave. "Talk to me, man," Tony insisted, running to shut the door.

Wordlessly, Matt reached under a pillow, holding aloft a pair of skimpy panties, matching Gina's tight pants. He opted to hang them from the unlit cigar while making a circuit around the room, high-fiving his cronies.

"Gina is, is….," Patrick politely ventured, puzzled.

"Easy what you say about my future wife," Matt chimed in. "But, why yes, I believe she is a certified professional courtesan."

Tony corrected him, somewhat offended. "Hey, court-a-what?" he said, slighted. "She may be easy, but, ya know, she ain't cheap. She can be classy and refined when she wants ta."

"And thanks to my buddy for life, Anthony Telesco, I'm no longer a virgin," Matt added, with bravado. "Jesus, the night I begin chemo again, I lose it. No shit."

"No shit," Pearl repeated, while Patrick looked at his roomies for confirmation.

"No shit," Tony repeated next.

"Shit," Patrick whispered, his mind now almost blank.

The three roommates piled on top of Patrick, wrestling, almost suffocating him. "And you're next," yelled Matt grinning, between the tangled bodies.

"Because she wants no part of Pearl," Tony added, muffling Patrick's protests with his enormous hairy hand.

"Bitch's afraid 15 minutes with me, and she'll only want dark chocolate for the rest her life," Pearl added, more boastful than slighted.

Patrick was clearly overmatched during the rowdiness. Not being able to fend off all three, he eventually submitted to the revelry.

"V-Day has arrived," Matt said, growing more excited.

"Rape," Patrick laughed between Tony's fingers. "Help. Rape."

One-by-one, they all felt a presence in the room, and one-by-one they stopped grappling, looking up toward the opened door. Tony's boy, back from errand running, stood at the entrance with Gina, his large mouth agape.

The "boy" was not a boy at all, Patrick assessed. In fact, he was a muscle-bound teen with a mean smile. His hair was cropped short. He wore loose black sweatpants, with a fitted gray tank top. Gracing his thick neck was a large pendant hung from one of five gold chains. Both wrists were surrounded by just as many bracelets and the bulging arms littered with colorful tattoos. Two six packs of Michelob were naturally tucked under each enormous arm.

"What da fuck ya doin'?" the comrade quizzed, his accent closer to Gina's than Tony's. "Yous looks like a homo on the bed."

Tony harshly banged a leg against the bedstand jumping off the bed. Limping away, he cautiously made introductions to Patrick. "Dis is Pete," he said.

The Hulk-like friend set down the spirits on a windowsill, still shell-shocked from what he had just witnessed. "Tony, look at ya hair," Pete said, irritated.

Tony walked over to the sink, repairing the temporary damage, while Pearl and Matt returned to their respective homesteads. Pete handed everyone a beer, except Pearl, an act noted by everyone.

The gigantic brute hopped into his wheelchair. "Ya mind?" he asked without asking.

Pete rolled away, leaving him stranded. "We'll give you a little privacy. Just don't ruin her," Tony said after dancing over with Gina.

Now captive in bed, Patrick's life felt to be unraveling at warp speed. It seemed like years ago when he was chilling with Edie on the roof, but now this beautiful evening was rapidly spiraling out of control.

Tony placed a condom, for precautionary purposes he said, in his palm, and then closed the curtain, only to then vanish. Matt's relentlessly playing radio sounded strangely distant as Gina took one last sip of beer before placing the glass bottle precariously close to the bedstand's edge. Like a magician, her short T-shirt went missing, exposing, for Patrick's eyes only, her exposed breasts.

Not wasting any time getting acquainted, a feisty Gina straddled and attacked him with a physical vengeance, shoving her long tongue down his throat, as if on a search-and-destroy military mission. Choking, Patrick shifted, temporarily freeing himself.

"So, so you used to babysit Tony," Patrick said, his mind racing. "Hah! I bet he was a wonderful…"

A libidinous Gina ended their one-sided conversation by cupping his head, and reinitiating her tongue's assignment. After placing Patrick's hands on her breasts, it finally dawned on him as to what was going to transpire, whether he wanted it to or not. His heart pounded as they continued kissing, Gina's roaming hands explored his body, roughly. Enticed, he no longer avoided the inevitable and reciprocated her kissing.

Without warning, Patrick heard several loud smashing sounds blending in with Pearl's scream. Startled by the reverberations, he pushed Gina aside. Instinctively, he went to transfer back into the wheelchair, but wisely stopped, mid-motion. At the last second, he remembered that Pete had absconded with it, making him virtually imprisoned in the bed.

Patrick tried regaining his balance, frantically pulling at the curtain, frightened by what he witnessed next. Pete held Pearl up against the wall, his body literally inches off the ground. The adamantine grip around Pearl's throat like a vice with one crutch smashed, the remnants strewn across the floor.

Tony was doing his best to calm his irate friend. "Whattaya doin'?" he commanded.

"Da nigga was lookin' at me funny," he shouted, insanely, blinded by animus.

Patrick scanned the room for his wheelchair, to no avail. In the meantime, Pete cocked his free hand and launched a blow directed at Pearl's face, who flinched. Suddenly, a quicker, hand intercepted the flying fist, causing the steroid abuser to stare at Tony in disbelief. Though straining, neither friend yielded.

"Get out," Tony said, violently. "Hear me? Get da fuck outta here."

"Wha?" Pete said, dumbfounded by the act of disloyalty, but releasing Pearl anyway.

Pearl crumpled to the ground like a damaged puppet, gasping for air. "Yous protectin' niggas ova ya buddies, now, Tony?" Pete continued.

"Ya deaf?" Tony said, upset. "Get da fuck out."

Hardened, Pete picked up the remaining beers, grabbed Gina like chattel, leaving before ensuring the lavender tee was properly in place. "Yous fucked up," Pete called out, storming toward the elevator, catching Benny's attention at the nursing station. Pearl lifted himself off the floor, leaned against the wall, rubbing his bruised neck. Tony picked-up the pieces to Pearl's broken staff, gently helping him to his bed.

"About my 'boy' ... I'm ... I'm," he tried to apologize.

Benny hurried into the room with two female nurses, carrying a tray full of tiny plastic cups, filled with various pills and liquid medications. He placed the tray near the sink, inspecting the messy room. He was also holding a syringe full of an odd-glowing fluid.

"You been drinkin' tonight, Matt-mon?" he quizzed, kicking an empty beer can.

"Come on," he said. "You know I never mix my drinking and chemo."

"Don't you boys be lettin' me down now," Voo-Doo Man barked. "Clean up this crap! Tony, that eye gets worked on tomorrow and Patrick, you have a bladder test first thing in the morning. Get some sleep and no more fluids."

He took the unlit cigar from Matt's mouth, wiped it clean, tucking it in his back pocket. He then closed the drape, tightly. As the others straightened the untidiness, Patrick watched the silhouettes behind the curtain. One shadow held the syringe, another a plastic bag filled with liquid, while Benny pressed down on Matt's shoulders, gently but firmly. The syringe's contents were injected into the plastic bag hanging from the ever present IV stand.

After several minutes, Matt cried out, his body convulsed, writhing in agony, while the shadows assisted in pinning their charge against the bed cushion. Feeling helpless, but yet respecting their roommate's remaining dignity, they left, allowing him to combat the pain alone. No one had remembered to turn off the radio before departing, though. The nighttime DJ, "Phantom Felix," commanded the ninety-ninth to call with the "Phrase That Pays."

Within seconds, however, Pearl re-entered the room using his remaining functional crutch. He headed to the windowsill, quickly scanned the medicine tray, putting numerous cups and their contents in his robe pocket. The temptation too powerful, his demons in total control, he couldn't care less if the nurses would have to later explain to immediate supervisors how the narcotics went missing.

§§§§

Father Burke carried in Communion as Patrick slept. However, the priest failed to notice the slumbering patient. He continually pecked his lips with the Eucharist, but then carelessly bent too far over, dropping the chalice on Patrick's face, awakening him with a start.

"What the…," Patrick began, but stopped.

"It slipped out of my hands."

"Excuse me, Father, I didn't know," he said, retrieving the fallen offerings from his bedding. "I'm having tests this morning, so I can't receive."

The elderly clergyman clumsily made his way out, still leaving much of the host strewn on the sheets. "God, what's wrong with him?" Patrick said aloud.

§§§§

By mid-morning, Patrick found himself on a hard, chilly X-ray table, in a gloomy, sparse windowless room, a borrowed thin, pale red hospital gown covering his torso. His anxiety escalating, he stared straight up, looking at metal emergency sprinklers popping out from the ceiling tiles. A zombie-looking fourth-year urology resident was prepping to shoot a massive quantity of contrast into his arm. Patrick grew worrisome watching the young doctor yawn incessantly, concluding he was simply plumb tired, and speculating this could spell trouble.

He felt most vulnerable and trapped at these moments. Standard hospital procedures required Patrick, as well as all other patients, be transported for X-rays or tests via stretchers, regardless of their condition. However, for him it meant leaving his wheelchair and physical independence back in the hospital room. There were instances when he was abandoned for, what seemed like eternity, lying in the poorly lit corridor, waiting for a free room, technician or doctor, leaving him with a sense of defenselessness.

More often than not, the frontline hospital employees heeded little attention when passing his stretcher, preoccupied with completing their mundane tasks or gossiping about absent fellow co-workers with present fellow co-workers. Occasionally, he would politely inquire as to the remaining wait time, but if not blatantly ignored, he was treated with disdain by lazy staff, who appeared essentially unaffected by his plight.

Their insensitivity was striking to Patrick, especially since they were employed as hospital personnel...places where people typically needed help. They couldn't care less about his thirst, hunger or even bathroom needs while he was left waiting. It irked him that he was forced to be overly polite or gracious just to be treated with any kind of respect. Ultimately, he held out that politeness would attract the attention of a rare orderly who took their responsibilities seriously.

In the overall scheme of things, though, this morning was moving smoothly. Patrick waited just two hours in the hallway before this sterile room became available. Once transferred to this space, he was left alone for only 45 additional minutes.

The young doctor had gone straight from a twenty-four hour call to his assigned urology shift and appeared to be sorely in need of a shave and shower. His facial hair exceeded a five o'clock shadow, while his green surgical uniform was partially tucked and beyond wrinkled. The three or four cat naps he snuck in did little to fend off the fatigue slowly dominating his body and more importantly, brain functions.

Grievously overworked, he was already idly daydreaming about his apartment's king bed, with the recently purchased box spring and top-of-the-line mattress. Once this procedure was finished, he would be soundly sleeping on it, though alone. Like his fellow residents, the doctor possessed great disdain for these long stretches of no sleep.

The doctor was aware this tricky medical procedure required his full attention. He was a bit disconcerted because had it not been for Michelle, the attractive, young tech assistant, the one he was positioning to ask out for dinner, he would have surely overslept. It must have been fate, he tiredly concluded, having Michelle stumble upon him snoozing in the seldom-used north stairwell. His mind began drifting to the tech's face, neck, legs, hands, and breasts.

"I'm positive Dr. Goodman did not want me to have an IVP," Patrick said, skeptically. "I'm here for a sonogram."

Partly startled and annoyed by the challenge, this teenager snapped him back to reality and away from what was transpiring into lewd mental R-rated images. The physician knew he had to concentrate on the task at hand...right after one more yawn.

"What's your name?"

"Dr. Martin," he replied, scantly listening. "Relax, the chart said IVP. I need to inject this dye so your bladder will show up on the X-rays."

Dr. Martin made a half-hearted gesture toward several charts tucked in a metallic bin affixed to the wall adjacent to the room entrance. The dead-tired doctor then realized he was not entirely certain where he placed the medical info for this patient, but he was almost certain it was the one he had just placed in the front of the others stuffed in the bin. But again he needed to concentrate, the young doctor kept reminding himself between constant suppressed yawns. Martin tied a thick, dull orange rubber hose around Patrick's arm, feeling for a viable vein.

He continued trying to persuade the doctor he was mistaken. "I'm telling you I had a reaction to the dye last year," he insisted vehemently. "Call my doctor."

Martin briskly blew off the comment, doing his best to stifle another yawn. "Yeah, yeah, yeah," he said, imperiously. "He's on his way."

"You're making a mistake, man," Patrick protested as the needle penetrated his bulging vein. "A big, big mistake."

"Listen, kid, I've been working for 28 hours straight, so cut me some slack and be quiet," he said rotely, finishing the injection, sounding more tired than annoyed. "I'm the doctor, not you."

Any other time and Patrick would have challenged Martin on his bedside manner and competence, but for now, already feeling queasy, he trained his eyes on the needle being pulled from his body.

To Patrick's chagrin, the resident began preparing a second syringe with a peculiar tiny needle. "I'm going to do an ABG while we wait for the dye to reach your bladder," Martin said, his impatience escalating.

"A, B, what?" Patrick replied, incredulous, keenly aware something was amiss. "Why?"

"I want to measure your blood's oxygen," Martin said, tremulously searching for an artery in the wrist as Patrick's legs inexplicitly began to spasm.

"Hold steady," Dr. Martin said stubbornly, more for his own benefit. "Calm down."

Martin found the artery, injected, momentarily preoccupied when Patrick's legs jumped, breaking the needle still in his wrist. Dr. Martin, wild-eyed, and speedily wide awake, knew he was abruptly over his head, medically.

"Oh shit," the young doctor exclaimed, feeling feckless and looking stunned, backing away, syringe still in hand, his mind racing through all options.

"My wrist," he screamed, a multi-colored rash quickly appearing first on his arms, then shoulders and chest before spreading to his legs.

"Oh shit," Martin kept repeating, bewildered. "Oh shit."

"Get my doctor," Patrick moaned, scratching his head and body with his needle-free hand. "Get any doctor, you moron."

"Don't touch anything," Martin said, vainly trying to keep some semblance of control.

The doctor hauled ass out of the room leaving Patrick alone, holding onto the table with his good arm, teeth clenched. Unnerved, he focused heavily on the needle and door, his breathing hastened as his body reddened and swelled. After waiting what seemed too long for Martin's return, he realized the severity of the situation. Patrick decided to take responsibility of the troublesome predicament. Reaching for the needle jutting from his wrist, he swiftly extracted it, throwing it to the floor. Like an exploded oil rig, blood began spurted from the punctured wound. Efforts to cap the blood with his hand, proved ineffectual as blood seeped through the pressing fingers.

Patrick, now looking like a ripe tomato, beckoned for help, moments before Dr. Goodman burst into the room, with Dr. Martin on his heels. The senior physician, logically and instinctively, began treating Patrick's wrist.

"This happened right after you injected dye?" Dr. Goodman boomed at the now adrenalin-powered Dr. Martin. "Did you even read the chart? It said no IVP and I did not order an ABG."

"Get me .5 mg of Epi," Dr. Goodman bellowed the simple instructions, throwing the chart in the direction of Dr. Martin. "Stat."

"Doctor," Patrick moaned, his agony worsening by the second.

Knowing he was likely to be held culpable for this mishap, Martin nippily handed Dr. Goodman the requested medication, who quickly administered it. "You are having an allergic reaction," he gently told a frightened Patrick. "The medication will make you feel better but it will also put you to sleep. When you wake up, you will be fine. I promise."

The injection zapped Patrick of any remaining energy, allowing him to painlessly drift away.

§§§§

On a bright, sunny day, people ate pre-made sub heroes, drank soda from long-neck glass bottles at a community picnic, while young children played baseball or frolicked around a swing set off in the distant. Patrick watched himself, laughing and throwing water balloons at friends.

He noticed a college-aged kid sneak up behind a pretty woman, pouring a cup of icy water down the back of her loose summer dress. She playfully cried out, turning to face her assailant; the young woman was Mary, smiling at the guy, chasing him with a full cup...revenge. They playfully wrestled, tumbling to the ground, but during the tussle she transformed into Gina. Slowly, they begin to kiss and as they did, she morphed once again, this time to Edie.

Alarmed, Patrick noticed an approaching auto, out of control, driving onto the field where the children played baseball. The car slammed its brakes but still hit a young boy standing alone in centerfield.

The car's impact vaulted the child through the air, eliciting Patrick to silently scream as he watched the youngster's body slam toward the ground.

§§§§

Patrick's eyes opened.

Feeling light-headed, it took several moments before realizing he was back in his hospital room. His body tingled, but he could sense the sensation waning. The thoughts of the picnic seemed too realistic, which startled him. Obviously, it was a dream he recognized, one he had two or three time a year. Whenever awakening, the bleak ending continually left him disillusioned and depressed.

He noted Tony and Pearl were lounging on his bed, both munching on a family-sized bag of Wise potato chips, chasing them down with cans of 7-Up. Matt sat in Patrick's wheelchair, absurdly wearing Gina's panties on his head like a skull cap, his long blond hair flowing from the elastic edges. Even Benny leaned against Tony's bed chewing on the recently confiscated unlit cigar. For no apparent reason, Patrick's space had become the room's de facto hang-out area.

They were playing poker together, using condoms as chips, a prominent stacked pile existed between Patrick's legs. Tony threw down his hand onto the bedsheets.

"Two pairs, Jacks high."

As he leaned in to pull the pot of condoms toward him, Patrick noticed the injured eye was covered with a fresh white gauze bandage in place of the usual black one. By the look of the number of condoms stacked in front of Tony, he concluded the Italian had won practically every hand. He silently chuckled that the fastidious kid from Brooklyn had his winning condoms divided in neat piles based on colors and brands.

"Ya shoudda kept dose three fives, ya know," said the poker know-it-all, while Pearl simply shrugged, absently doodling with borrowed crayons on a borrowed legal pad, his mouth full of junk food. Amazing, potato chip oil- stained intricate drawings of vibrant, fictitious comic book characters were strewn on his bed and floor, indicating the sketch session had been a long one. Patrick had no idea of Pearl's possessed artistic talent.

"What's going on?" Patrick said hoarsely, finally becoming oriented to his surroundings.

They all jumped, not noticing he had awaken, the roommates struggled to conceal they had been worried.

"Hey, Sleeping Beauty," Matt said, plaintively. "Tony's teaching Pearl how to play poker. And Pearl is instructing us all on how not to draw stick figures."

Pearl put down a navy blue crayon to slowly shuffle the deck of cards. As usual, a radio played in the background. Tony winked at Patrick while counting his additional winnings, accidentally dropping a Trojan between the mattress and bedframe. He frantically searched the floor for the condom, when Patrick vaguely noticed the tray full of medicine on the windowsill across from his bed. Voo-Doo Man was obviously taking an extended break before dispensing the prescribed medicines.

"Just a friendly game," Tony said in a seasoned manner, clutching the errant winning in his left hand.

"Patrick, it looked like ya was trippin', man," Pearl said.

"Ok, I'll admit it, you had us all worried," Matt added.

"I feel like I was just hit by a car," Patrick responded, wearily, the words instantly jarring him, but no one else within earshot.

"What happened to your eye?" Patrick asked, moments after Pearl began clumsily dealing the next hand.

"My eye?"

"The new patch, moron," he replied, pointing to his fresh bandage.

"Oh yeah, pretty cool, huh?" Tony answered. "Guess da fuck what? My doc said the cosmetic procedure was a success. I'm gettin' out tomorrow. I'll even be able to see outta da eye in a couple of weeks."

Finally finished dealing, the players intently inspected their cards. A scowl crossed Benny's face, causing him to absently bite tighter into the cigar, Pearl looked lost, and Matt seemed completely disinterested in the game.

"Give me four," Benny ordered.

"Three," Matt said, nonchalantly.

Tony appeared satisfied with his hand. "I'll play dese," he declared.

"I need five," Pearl said, tentatively.

Tony became annoyed at his pupil. "No, no Pearl. Four's da limit," he said.

"Uh, okay. I'll just give myself one," he countered, sticking his hand deep into the near empty bag of chips, while Tony rolled his eyes.

"Hey, Patrick, your dad called when you were under," Matt informed him.

"Yeah, what did he want?" he asked, attempting to sound indifferent. "Did he know about the test SNAFU?"

"He was askin' if ya braces worked," Tony interrupted. "I think he wants to come visit."

"Shit," Patrick said annoyed.

Pearl looked up from his cards, stuffing the last of the munchies into his mouth. "You don't want him to?" he asked.

Patrick acted tougher. "Hey, I see my dad enough at home," he said avoiding all eyes.

Benny grimaced and tossed down his hand. He removed the cigar from his mouth, the end now saturated with saliva, grabbing his last remaining condom. Not that he needed any birth control, but he disliked losing. The nurse decided to take a 15-minute break, thinking the game would be a painless killing. Instead, he purchased twenty contraceptives for the lone 20 bucks in his wallet to join the game, and a half an hour later, he angrily found himself without drinking money for tonight.

"I'm out," he barked, departing the game and room, forgetting the waiting tray of medications.

"I'm raising the pot three Trojans," Matt said.

"Alright, but here's two more," Tony said, upping the ante. "That's five to ya, Pearl."

"Five?" he pondered aloud, first scoping the unprotected tray of drugs, then the small pile of packets, and finally at Tony's mountain of winnings. "Hmm, fine. I'll raise it five."

"Five more?" Matt asked, wandering over to his bed. "I quit."

"I'll see dat five and here's everything else," Tony said, looking menacingly at his pigeon, carefully placing every possessed converted chip into the pot. "You can owe me."

"Can you do that?" Pearl wondered.

"Sure," Tony replied. "No vig on the debt either."

"Well, I don't know what the fuck a vig is," Pearl complained. "But here's my last Rough Riders."

Tony placed down his cards, confidently reaching for the waiting pot, forcing Pearl to cringe. "My man, I got a straight," Tony said.

"Gee, I only got a pair of ones and another pair of ones," Pearl countered, after pausing.

"Ones?" Tony asked, freezing, underestimating the caliber of his opponent.

Pearl steadily placed down his cards. Four aces. "Sucker," Pearl exclaimed.

Tony sulked when the victorious roommate plowed the entire loot to his side of the bed. Aghast, he had been taken by the presumed neophyte, fleeced for the first time. Although initially shocked, Tony had no choice but to admire Pearl's balls. Patrick was unsure if Tony was more upset at losing the prize or having to watch Pearl mess up the strategically organized piles.

Pearl slid the grudging Tony a condom. "In case you get lucky tonight, Stallion," he said.

After a moment, Tony laughed, and the others quickly followed. Patrick pulled out a Pepsi six-pack and box of Yodels, offering them to everyone. The Brooklynite stood, good-naturedly ribbing Pearl, but then began to trim his sideburns with professional salon scissors when leaning over the sink.

"About tonight, if ya think ya're hot shit now, know ya're buyin' tonight," Tony said.

"Buyin' what?" Pearl said, unsure where the thought process was heading.

"Da beers, man, ya know," Tony continued, now beginning to methodically lay out street clothes on his bed, holding a black tapered fine silk shirt up to the light.

"Ya think I'm gonna spend my last night in this room?! We're outta here."

"Can't go," Matt said, simply. "Chemo."

"Ya feel up to it, Patrick?" Tony asked.

Wow, Patrick thought. Sneaking out of the hospital would have serious repercussions, if caught. The idea of taking an unauthorized leave had never crossed his mind. But then, what was the worst thing that could happen? The hospital would tell his parents? They would send him home? He would bear the wrath of Sister Margaret or Dr. Goodman? From a cost-benefit-analysis, these were all acceptable punishments. He was tired of always playing by the rules, being the obedient one, taking the safest course of actions. Besides, he had always wanted to roam the surrounding neighborhood. It was a silly question he concluded and started changing his attire.

Looking dapper, Tony slipped into his couture clothes, eventually admiring himself with a handheld mirror. Patrick's outfit was a bit more natural, consisting of a powder-blue hoodie sweatshirt, white Levi jeans, and his favorite weathered tan cowboy boots. Pearl changed into the same ragged clothes he wore when admitted; an off-white long sleeve T-shirt, stained khakis, and high top black sneakers with tattered laces.

Patrick absently began singing along to The Chi-Lites tune playing on the radio. "One month ago today, I was happy as a lark," surprisingly on key. "But now I go for walks, to the movies, maybe to the park."

Pearl, knowing the words, too, joined him in unison, "And I have a seat on the same old bench, to watch the children play. You know, tomorrow is their future, but to me, it's just another day."

Matt added vocals to the popular hit after turning the radio volume to maximum. "They all gather around me, they seem to know my name. We laugh, tell a few jokes, but it still doesn't ease my pain."

Even Tony could not resist being part of the impromptu group, surprising everyone with having memorized the lyrics to a song not popular in his neck of the woods. "I know I can't hide from a memory, though day after day I tried. I keep sayin' she'll be back, but today again I lied."

All four formed a single line in the room, Matt rolled up a thick Penthouse magazine to act as a microphone while they all belted out the song, attempting synchronized, rhythmic, dance moves. Their voices resonated throughout the floor and down the hallway, ultimately drawing an ever growing crowd of nurses, patients, visitors, and doctors into their oversized room, all wanting to witness the crooning quartet. As the song progressed, each of the roommates moved front and center, grabbing the makeshift microphone, performing their amateurish act surprisingly well.

When it was Pearl's turn, he ignored the "microphone" and instead gracefully picked up his roomie's guitar, playing an unrehearsed solo. His long fingers naturally slid up and down the instrument's neck, his professional playing skills making Patrick seem like an amateur. An artist, musician, who knew this kid from the streets was a potential prodigy?

When the music finally ended, the room exploded with applause from the unexpected audience. The spectators cheered the teamwork, eventually dispersing back to their respective rooms and work areas, Pearl cradling the guitar like a baby.

"Hey, here's something for you guys tonight," Matt said, calling Pearl over to his bed, generously slipping bills into his hand. "Have a good time on me."

Before the others noticed, Pearl stuffed the money into one of his front pockets. A stand-in 99X DJ, "Happy Howie," interrupted the commotion in the room by asking for the ninety-ninth caller. Like a madman, Matt lunged for the nearest room phone, almost ripping the IV hanger from his arm.

"Wait, you guys," Matt said, franticly. "Man the phones. They want the 99th caller."

Tony and Patrick started dialing the station on the two remaining outdated rotary phones while Pearl, not having one, simply pulled the money out of his pocket to discover Matt had given him three $100 bills. This time, he concealed the money in his waistband as the others proceeded with the dialing, only to hear busy signals at the other end. They all continued dialing, furiously. Busy again. Dial/busy. Dial/busy. Matt was the first to begin tiring.

"It's no use," he said, dejectedly.

An excited look came over Patrick's face. "It's ringing," he screamed.

"That's happened to me before," Matt countered, wearily. "Trust me, no one is going to pick-up."

"What's the Phrase That Pays?" Happy Howie asked flippantly after answering the phone, causing Patrick to wildly fling his free arm back and forth trying to get his Matt's attention.

"Hold on a second," he said, trying to stall, realizing he never did quite know the phrase.

Patrick looked over to Matt, pointing at his phone, pleading. "What is it?" he demanded. "What is the phrase?!"

"Shit, I have no idea," Matt cried, embarrassed to admit he had no clue, either.

"I love 99X," he guessed, now on his own.

While the others were distracted with the call, Pearl jumped over to the medical tray, taking two recognizable opiate pills, swallowing them without water, and tossing away the empty plastic pill container.

"Nope," Happy Howie, responded, sounding quickly bored.

"99X is the best station," Patrick said, grasping.

"No," Howie said, a fearful Patrick certain the DJ would hang up and take another call. How could anyone in the room, especially, Matt, not know the phrase they heard uttered 1,000 times this past week?

Luckily it was near the end of Happy Howie's shift, so he decided to throw the caller a lifeline. "Did I just hear you say 99X is my favorite radio station?" the DJ asked.

"Yeah, what did you think I said?" Patrick bluffed, thankful for the leading question.

"Okay, you're our winner," Howie announced. "Where are you calling from and what record do you want?"

Patrick sensed an opportunity, deciding to pull out and play his ever-waiting violin for full affect. "Welllll, I'm from upstate New York, but right now I'm a patient at St. Jude's Hospital in the Village," he dramatically informed the radio personality.

The DJ's interest was piqued. "St. Jude's?" he asked. "What's the matter with you?"

"Skiing," he commented, knowing he hooked the radio personality. "Junior Olympic Ski Team. Colorado. The cliff. You probably read about it."

Patrick now had Happy Howie's full attention.

§§§§

Huddled against a wall, Pearl, Tony and Patrick were a mere five yards from the nurses' station in the midst of their great escape as on the staff radio "Happy Howie" talked over a song's opening.

"This one goes out to Pearl, Patrick, Tony, Matt and their 16 ward mates at St. Jude's. 99X is going to hand-deliver a box full of albums and T-shirts for being the city's biggest rock fans. Here's the song they all wanted to hear, 'For the Love of Money'."

§§§§

Benny sipped stale coffee from a chipped Styrofoam cup, standing alone in front of the elevator bank reading a passed around copy of the New York Post. He still steamed from the loss of poker money, but concluded the offered overtime tonight would alleviate his guilt and his need to connect with buddies for drinks.

The three escape artists made a steady pace down the hallway before ducking into a nearby linen closet as Benny's attention wavered. He folded up the paper, tucking it into his armpit and walked toward Tito's room.

Patrick quickly realized the closet lacked a light switch, forcing them to patiently wait in the tight dark box for the precise time to crack the door open. Guessing correctly, Patrick found the hallway empty when finally peering out. The roommates took the fortuitous opportunity to jump out of the small confines to rush toward the elevators. However, the wait for one seemed like an eternity, as all three nervously looked down the corridor.

Benny looked in on the sleeping Tito and five other toddlers who all were sound asleep in stainless steel cribs. Tito slept with a peaceful look, his new stuffed panda resting next to his angelic face. The nurse could not contain his idiosyncratic cleanliness tendencies, picking up the various plastic toys scattered around the floor.

The three amigos continued waiting for an elevator, not being able to pry their eyes away from the floor indicators. Pearl and Tony scrunched their bodies against the exterior elevator doors, hoping to conceal themselves, while bestowing Patrick with "the Benny watch." Finally, the call light illuminated and rang as Benny exited Tito's room. But he suddenly stopped, looked back at the young patients, when one abruptly stirred.

The elevator, which Tony leaned on, opened, catching him off guard. He clumsily tumbled into the cab as it jolted in all directions. Pearl hesitated before jumping in assisting the embarrassed, roommate off the dirty floor. Staggering upright, Tony appeared to worry more about his hair and attire then any bodily injuries. Patrick rushed into the waiting vertical box, but not quickly enough as the closing door hit his chair, forcing it to reopen.

Benny finally exited Tito's room, but heard the elevator door's potential malfunction. Peering down the corridor, he saw emptiness, allowing him to refocus on the newspaper.

Inside the elevator, the three roommates felt the cab make its descending path. They nervously glanced at one another when it made an unexpected stop on the third floor, worried their ruse was prematurely over. It was apparent anything that could go wrong, actually did. The thought crossed Patrick's mind to admit defeat, change direction, and return to the room's safe harbor. When the doors finally opened, a building janitor entered, dragging an aged and battered bucket. Doing their best not to make visual contact, the elevator continued its flight after the new occupant pressed the basement button.

The janitor, whistling what sounded like Dean Martin's, "That's Amore," deliberately eyed his three temporary neighbors. Pearl nervously smiled at Patrick who in turn looked pleadingly at Tony.

Yes, Tony too, calculated the risks, but he never anticipated things to go awry so quickly. At the worst, he thought some young, errant New York City police officer would request appropriate identification somewhere outside the hospital confines, but even that worry was a stretch. This new passenger was an aberration.

"Boy, that nurse was tough," Tony inexplicitly, blurted. "I told you guys we'd get in trouble for stayin' past visitin' hours."

The elevator soon stopped at the lobby floor, allowing the roomies to take flight. The kindly janitor shook his head, laughing to himself, changing his whistling to humming. The hospital employee knew what the fleeing occupants were up to, but the nightly responsibilities had precedent.

Looking around, the roommates found themselves in a surprisingly stuffy, barren lobby. Tony spotted a lone, massive security guard sitting behind a plain, metal desk next to the rear building entrance. His girth strained the strength of the provided matching metal folding chair. The guard's disheveled blue uniform had prominent, if not permanent, sweat stains around the shirt collar and under each armpit. He incessantly scratched the pronounced red blotches on his swollen hands.

"Watch da masta in action," Tony said assertively.

The Italian Stallion strutted over to the lonely man, who lovingly nursed Hershey candy bars and Dr. Pepper. A circular fan stationed behind the desk, blew targeted gusts scattering the few strands of intermittent head hair, across his sweaty face. He had thought of calling in sick this evening to watch the Yankees play the Red Sox, now in extra innings, with buddies who held day jobs. The lack of accrued personal time necessitated the game be viewed on the tiny portable black-and-white television he purchased with the weekend and midnight-to-eight security guards. He strained, trying to make out the scratchy figures on the screen. What these strangers wanted was beyond him, but his late night snack and ball game warranted his full attention.

"Mista, can you tell me where's da emergency room?" Tony asked over the loud fan.

Sensing the unresponsive guard did not hear the question, he repeated it, this time with hands cupped around his mouth. As Tony dragged out the fictitious directional conversation with the guard, Patrick and Pearl disappeared into the street lamp lit sidewalks. Tony feigned understanding the bellowed instructions over the buzzing and loud television. He nodded, pointed toward the door, before remembering the exposed blue ID wrist bracelet. The patient deftly put the arm behind his back, nodded, thanking the guard, before exiting the building – to the waiting paradise.

They wandered afoot along the crowded Village streets and avenues, window watching various stores and scoping passing people. Patrick was in awe, his eyes open wide, absorbing the Village's vibrancy. Honking car horns, street peddlers, and unrecognizable food fragrance all commanded his attention. This was the first, and perhaps only time, he would be able to experience the city's nightlife.

They entered a local bar, crowded with patrons who were obviously into leather. A tormented Tony nervously looked around at the patrons wearing leather items with a combined cowboy and motorcycle theme. He made a hasty retreat, while Pearl and Patrick only shrugged, eventually following their roommate out.

Back on the sidewalks, Patrick patiently wheeled by a seasoned homeless person curled on a park bench – his designated homestead. The destitute man was protected by shopping carts overflowing with plastic bags of empty aluminum cans and bottles. A runt mutt was asleep next to its unemployed master, his head on the man's lap, as Patrick quietly placed a few spare quarters in a nearby bowl, however, the man appeared more insolent than grateful after viewing the donation total.

At a corner several blocks away, the roomies bought and consumed large, salty pretzels from a grimy street vendor, harsh smoke billowing from the cart. They each loaded mustard on the brick-hard pieces of expired baked dough.

They passed an outdoor, professional modeling shoot taking place in a long, narrow alleyway. They stopped to watch a thin, male hairdresser hastily dry an equally emaciated blond Russian female model's hair with two blow dryers. They chose to continue their excursion after receiving threatening glares from the photo shoot team. Not far away, they stumbled upon park performers rapping and break dancing. Tony ran into a McDonald's to purchase milkshakes for everyone.

Patrick was in awe of the diverse sightings. This was unlike anything he ever experienced. His previous night outings consisted of seeing movies, going to a local pizzeria, attending a school basketball game or swimming meet. They all paled in comparison to what he was now digesting.

They hailed a yellow cab, taking them to the Staten Island Ferry Dock at Battery Park. Hitching a ride, they overlooked the dark water, enjoying their freedom as the foul-smelling air raced against their faces, helping them forget about their hospital obligations.

After the ferry returned them to Manhattan, Patrick stopped and parked his wheelchair next to the center fountain at Washington Square Park while Tony and Pearl pressed forward. Sucking up the remaining shake from the large waxed paper cup, a middle-aged couple strolled by, stopping unexpectedly in front of him.

With visible pity, the man pulled-out a silver money clip from his sport coat inside pocket, removed a crisp $5 bill, placing it into the now empty, but still damp, cup. Patrick looked peculiarly at the lone bill, then at the clothes he was wearing, then finally back at the couple as they walked away. Without having a chance to protest, he pocketed the over-the-top voluntary donation. This night was truly turning out to be memorable he thought, before pushing his wheelchair toward his roomies.

§§§§

Matt was still lying in his hospital bed when Benny walked in with the same nurses from the previous injection carrying the chemo needle and plastic bags filled with dark colored drugs.

"Where are those three roomies of yours?" Benny said swabbing his arm.

"Uh, I think they, they went to the patio, to, to give me space," he replied, trying not to sound defensive while ignoring the needle and reinforcements.

§§§§

Traveling at a steady pace, the trio passed a man selling flowers on the sidewalk edge, when Pearl detected several transparent drug dealers in a remote brownstone doorway, exchanging tinfoil packets of heroin after completing elaborate, multi-layered transactions. Still feeling flush from the recently ingested opiates, an urge overpowered the crutch-supported young boy. Flush with Matt's funds, he moved away from his small posse to make a score.

Tony heard loud R&B/Soul music blaring from a nearby club. "Let's check out dis place," he whooped while Patrick followed him to the bar.

Pearl purposefully lingered behind. "I'll catch up," Pearl called out, eying the lowlife peddlers. Reluctantly, conceding to his neurological cravings, he convinced himself this one would truly be the last purchase. Until this week, he had been clean for over three months, a record for this addict.

As Tony and Patrick neared the club, Pearl made a pretend beeline for the flower guy, but as he neared, he pulled out one of the $100 bills, altered directions, in pursuit of a profligate transaction.

§§§§

Tony and Patrick managed to ease their way through the club crowd, beers in hand, when they passed a clearly intoxicated, knockout redhead with uncommonly big breasts and lipstick in dire need of some refreshing. Tony, like a lion targeting prey, instantly sensed that if played correctly, this woman would provide an enjoyable evening.

"Hi, I'm Jennifer," she slurred, nursing the end of a longneck Budweiser and holding a near-finished cigarette. "What happened to you, Ironside?"

Sitting at the table were two other women who looked to be identical twins wearing matching Bruce Springsteen "Born in the USA" concert T-shirts. Various empty beer bottles accumulated their tabletop partnered by a butt-filled ashtray. In a flash, the natty Tony plopped in an empty chair between the twins, surveying the options.

"Skydiving," Patrick responded, sounding natural. "The Empire State Building. You probably read about it."

Pearl finally entered the club's front door, using his crutches, he slowly ambled around the groups of people, holding colored tulips in one hand. Feeling the drug-induced rush, he spotted his unsuspecting buddies at the table. Pearl grabbed a spare chair from a nearby table, rested his support gear against the small table, sat next to Jennifer, and handed her the flower arrangement.

"For me?" Jennifer asked.

Pearl winked at the guys, just as Edie appeared from the crowd, pressing three fresh beers against her body. Walking toward the table, she recognized Patrick.

"Oh my God," she happily cried out, shining.

"Edie," Patrick said, surprised by the encounter, noticing sweat dripping down her neck only to be absorbed by a skimpy white tank top contrasting against her tanned skin.

"I was only gone three minutes and look who took my chair," she said, eying Tony.

Tony jumped up apologetically, grabbing one last available nearby chair for Edie. She placed the bottles on the table top when Patrick, surprising himself, noted her engagement band was missing, a half-inch wide of noticeably white skin circling a tanned ring finger. It was probably the first time he had ever purposely checked for a wedding/engagement ring. Was that a sign of getting older, he wondered?

Before he could give that question further consideration, the intoxicated redhead grabbed his arm. "You know these guys, Edie?"

"Sure do," Edie interjected. "What're you doing here, Patrick?"

"Lookin' for fine college women like y'all," Pearl said before the roommate could answer.

"Well we're lookin' for hot, young guys like y'all," Jennifer said, sipping beer from one of the replacement bottles.

Patrick glanced at Edie, who he discovered was closely observing. Their eyes locked, without either uttering a word, the already unspoken lure only intensified. They both hoped to deflect the mutual attraction by encouraging distracting dialogue.

"C'mon, let's dance," the unsuspecting Tony screamed, when an Earth, Wind & Fire song cued from the DJ booth.

"Sure," said one of the twins, as Tony yanked both sisters onto the dance floor.

Pearl stood on one crutch, looking at Edie's intoxicated, frisky, redheaded friend, seeking permission. "Ma'am, may I have the honor of your company on the dance floor?" Pearl asked, using flawless manners when offering an arm.

"Why not?" said Jennifer, as Pearl left the second crutch at the table, making it easier for them to make their way to the crowded, sweltering dance floor.

"Patrick, order some decent champagne," he commanded before scampering. "It's on Matt."

"Two hundred bucks?" he exclaimed after seeing the bills magically appear on the table.

"Yeah, not bad," Pearl shouted back, disappearing with Jennifer, an arm around her firm hips.

Since she had nothing to do with Patrick's escape, Edie figured there was no impropriety in enjoying one drink with him. This decision probably violated various codes of ethics, but dammit, she too wanted to let go for once. Enjoy the moment, this night Edie demanded to herself.

This was the first time seeing Patrick in street clothes, she further thought, her mind forgetting any age difference.

"I can't believe you snuck out," Edie said, taking a swig of beer, sliding into a chair next to Patrick, trying to hear better. "You are all crazy, but hilarious. If you are killed tonight doing something illicit, I'll deny ever seeing you."

"What would you like?" a young waitress, wearing a one-piece black mini dress, asked Edie, appearing out of thin air.

"I guess a bottle of vintage champagne," Edie said, displaying the double Benjamin Franklins.

The waitress warily regarded Patrick and the wheelchair, immediately looking back at Edie. This guy reminded her of a high school classmate who lost both legs screwing around on the subway, only to have him fall between two train cars; except this patron was better looking and apparently less disabled. But, regardless, the wheelchair made her nauseous.

"Would he like something else?" she inquired, indecisively.

Edie glared at the waitress, with daggers displayed. "Oh, he can order for himself," she said agitated, trying to control herself. "What would you like, Little Pat?"

She coyly gave Patrick a look, clasping her warm, smooth hand in his, causing a bolt to rush throughout his body, even the paralyzed limbs. Taking her cue, he faked a complete body spasm pretending to have a severe case of CP. Patrick's sudden jumping about, made the waitress look pale and faint, and simply wanting to evaporate from the scene. He jerked, pointing at his unofficial date.

"He'll have the same," she said to the suddenly passive waitperson, who slowly backed away from the scene, before finally running toward the bar's sanctuary. Her reaction only made the troublemakers burst out with hysterical laughter.

The song ended, morphing into another by Harold Melvin & The Blue Notes. Patrick and Edie shouted in unison, "The Love I Lost."

"Wanna dance?" she begged.

"Really?"

Patrick swerved his way to the middle of the frenzied, swaying crowd, popping wheelies along the way as they danced together. Other interested patrons in the lounge area walked toward the dance floor to initially watch but then to encourage the act on, a wide circle formed around the duet, cheering and goading.

Tony, Pearl, Jennifer and the twins, clapped in unison at the dancing couple. Eventually, they all decided to leave the packed dancing area for the bar, now completely empty, ordering tequila shots, instantly pumping them down, using the liquor to narcotize any remaining anxieties. As they ordered a second round, the bartender, with unnaturally highlighted blond hair, thought about his already tired legs and aching feet, but noticed the wide, blue ID bracelets Pearl and Tony wore on their respective wrists.

"Hey, your bracelets," he barked, cryptically. "St. Jude's, right?"

"Listen, man, I, I can..," Pearl said, thinking they would be escorted out and back to the medical center.

"At this bar, St. Jude bracelets mean two-for-one," the bartender surmised, not requiring an explanation. Tony, Pearl and the women hugged each other as the barkeep poured everyone free shots.

"I love ya, man," Tony said to Pearl after downing the additional liquid, feeling the alcohol warm his body.

"No, I really love ya, man," he went on, putting his arm around Pearl's shoulder. "But not in, ya know, a homo kind of way, ya know?"

He decided to take advantage of Tony's unexpected friendly behavior, snatching a quick, but loud kiss on his lips. Laughing, he speedily limped away from the homophobe, with Jennifer on his arm. Embarrassed, Tony looked over at the intrigued, wearied bartender, who eyed him suspiciously after overhearing and viewing the exchange, as were the twins, who both licked away the remains of the shots from their teeth.

"He was just kiddin', ya know Pearl, he's a funny guy," Tony said defensively. "Crazy guy. He was just yankin' my chain."

The unconvinced bartender smiled, shook his head, only to walk to the other end of the long bar in search of ripe tips.

Tony looked back toward the dance floor to see Edie and Patrick dancing in the middle of large open area, surrounded by nearly every patron. Patrick was clearly showing-off popping wheelies and quickly rotating, almost toppling over backwards. Fascinated with his presence, Edie sensed her moment to jump onto his lap and eliminate the distance between them, laughing as he performed complex wheelies and quick turns with an unanticipated passenger.

"I'm eighteen again," she yelled into his ear, pressing closer. "I haven't felt like this since..."

"You were eighteen," he finished, consuming her fragrance.

§§§§

The empty chemo syringe was inadvertently knocked to the floor as Benny and two other nurses held down a screaming Matt who vainly fought the chemotherapy drugs, once again. The male nurse placed himself on top of his writhing body, keeping the suffering teenager from propelling off the bed. Quite simply, Matt was crazed.

The extreme pain enabled Matt to overpower the assigned staff. Yes, he dreaded the chemo, but usually the drugs eventually knocked him out. But this dose was different and thus his reaction was atypical.

Thinking that only death could save him, Matt forced his mind to take him elsewhere, on a trip far away. Matt felt himself leave his body. He was floating over his body, repudiating the drugs, watching the activity engulf the hospital bed he occupied, allowing him to be a pain-free spectator. For the first time in a long time, he finally felt free.

§§§§

The club visitors gave the dancing couple a loud applause when the song ultimately ended. Many proceeded back to the bar and tables while others remained for the next tune, Al Green's "Let's Stay Together."

Patrick, though pumped, was amazed at how the dancing exerted him so. It must have been Edie's added weight, he quickly concluded because his hands, arms and shoulders felt the same blood rush when lifting. But he was exhilarated, never feeling happier.

"What do I owe you for the ride," a blushing Edie asked, still sitting on his lap, obviously affectionate.

"50 cents or a kiss," Patrick ventured.

Edie teasingly paused a moment before responding. "Got change for a dollar?" she asked, giving him a hug, feeling the perspiration emanating from his well-defined, upper body.

They hugged again, however, longer and harder than previously. Edie's hair was redolent of the smell of honeysuckle shampoo, as well as her warm, Champagne- flavored breath on his neck. Cheek-to-cheek, he gradually repositioned so their faces were inches apart.

Unexpectedly, Tony jumped in, spinning Patrick and Edie. Patrick's moment had been lost, he knew, but he beamed at Edie anyway as she allowed gravity to take control, leaning back, enjoying the fast, merry-go-round ride.

§§§§

The three slipped back into their room, their clothes reeking of cheap cigarettes and stale alcohol. Matt's labored breathing filled the room. His curtain was open, forcing them to quietly undress while still wasted. Pearl, trying to act sober, unsuccessfully attempted to lean his crutches against a bed in the dark, only to have them loudly crash to the uncarpeted floor. After the long unauthorized outing, all three were beyond tired.

Matt was actually awake listening to them clumsily undress. It had been a long night for him, too. Something unsettling, yet comforting, transpired which unnerved him in the way it clarified his waning battle with the cancer. This particular dosage was vicious in the manner it attacked. His stomach was ablaze and inflamed making the constant methadone drip feel like fighting a forest fire with a water pistol. Even his fingernails ached. The reappearance of the friends brought a smile to his face, though. He allowed himself to eavesdrop on Tony's somewhat slurred whispers about the night's dancing exploits. It sounded like his financial donation was put to good use during their outing.

"Fun time?" Matt shakily speculated, startling them.

Tony jumped out of his pants. "Jesus, ya scared the shit outta me," he said, momentarily. "I, we thought ya was asleep."

Wearing a new 99X red shirt, Matt pointed to a large box sitting on a window sill. "Patrick, your sob story with the DJ worked," Matt said sounding tired. "He had a station intern deliver the shirts and album right after you all left."

Pearl hopped over to the open box, pulling out various colored station T-shirts. Still in street clothes, Patrick climbed into bed while Tony filled the sink with cold water, submerging his entire face in the liquid for at least several seconds.

"How'd the chemo go?" Patrick asked.

"Never again," he replied, summarizing. "No more chemo."

Matt raised a white hand towel and waved it like a surrender flag, chucking it at Tony as he lifted his face from the cold water, droplets dripping to the floor. Pearl skipped past holding a few selected T-shirts and albums.

"Ya can't give up, Matty," Tony said, wiping off the excess water with the towel.

"Fuck you," Matt countered, suddenly irked. "You don't know what you're talking about. I'm taking a walk to the porch. Get some of that fresh New York City air. How's that for an oxymoron?"

Matt laughed at his own joke, Tony looking more trashed than confused, did not respond, wanting only to find an available mattress. Patrick sat on his bed listening and watching the quick exchange.

"Want some company, Matt?" Patrick asked.

"Nah," Matt said, quickly. "You guys must be dead."

Matt worked his way out of bed, dragging the IV walker along the floor. But before exiting, he stopped, pulling off his blond, straight hair, exposing a shiny, bald, Mr. Clean head. He tossed the wig at Pearl, hitting him squarely.

"What the fuck," Pearl yelled, jumping as if hit by a flea-infested blanket. "You a wild, white boy."

"It's real?" Tony asked.

"It's real fake hair," Matt replied.

"The hair's fake," Tony sneered. "What else, ya know, on your body is fake?"

"Only Gina knows," Matt advised with a malicious grin.

Pearl skipped to the sink mirror, checking himself out with the blond wig over his pronounced afro. Matt left the room, the squeaky sound of the dragging IV ultimately abated.

"You guys think someone should go with him?" Patrick asked to no one in particular.

"Don't know, don't care" Tony said, now in a prone position. "I'm goin' to sleep. Whatta fuckin' night, ya know. Shit, I'm gonna be hung over when I get picked up in the mornin'."

"I gotta take a piss," Patrick announced, as Pearl, still wearing the blond hair, reached into his nightstand, promptly hiding an unseen object among the other meager personal possessions.

§§§§

After flushing the toilet and washing his hands, Patrick tossed away the large paper cup he had just relieved himself into. Before squeezing through the narrow bathroom door, he slipped on the Walkman headphones amplifying the selected radio music.

When using the hallway restroom, it bothered him the hospital, of all places, failed to provide an accessible bathroom for wheelchair users who like everyone else, needed to use it on a more than daily basis. If he needed to urinate he would enter the small bathroom and use a stainless steel urinal, sometimes a cup if in dire straits. But the provided space was so confined, he was unable to close the door behind him, thus allowing passing staff and visitors to witness personal body functions. Not only was it incomprehensible, it was demeaning, to boot.

If it was bowel care-related, he would transfer onto the toilet allowing a nurse to take away his chair so the door could be shut for privacy. However, when he was finished, Patrick had to hope that nurse remembered he was stranded and waiting for the wheelchair to be returned. It was not unusual for him to have to yell for long periods of time before someone heard or remembered he was marooned.

Wheeling into the empty hallway, Patrick looked to his room, but impulsively, decided to head the opposite direction. Perhaps, he hoped, Matt would enjoy some company. For unexplained reasons, he had a premonition something was amiss.

Patrick reached the corner, stopped and looked outside the open deck door. Although not surprised to see his roommate, he was shocked to see a bald Matt perched on the porch railing, his back facing out. Patrick became instantly concerned after realizing the ever present IV had been disconnected. Trusting never-tested instincts, he tentatively moved closer to the porch and his friend. Matt, hearing the ruckus the wheelchair made maneuvering around the construction detritus, looked up.

"Hey, hey, hey, Matt," he said, trying to act casually.

"What's up?" he replied, sounding more upbeat than blasé.

"Get off the ledge, man," he gently instructed, trying to decipher why Matt was sitting on the rail, late at night, with his IV cast aside. "It's dangerous and I don't want you to get in trouble."

"I'm just tired of hurting, you know?" Matt said, innocently.

Patrick continued approaching, but the front wheels kept hitting pieces of loose debris and ill-placed tools.

"Tired?" Patrick asked, officially confused and worried. "Come on. You're scaring the shit out of me. Please get down."

"Stay where you are, Patrick," he commanded. "Don't come any closer."

"Matt," he angrily pleaded, his heart pounding.

"All I ever wanted was to go to college, meet a girl, and make babies."

"This is not making any sense."

As a violent cough erupted, Matt twisted to focus on the below patio floor. His words no longer were directed to Patrick, who carefully pressed forward.

"That's never going to happen," Matt said, about to list the various factors. "I know that now. Life is all about choices. Everything we do in life is a choice. Do I brush my teeth or shave first? Do I root for the Mets or the Yankees? Do I try chemo or radiation? Hah, like that's a fucking choice."

"Matt," Patrick could only say in despair. "Matt."

"I have no more choices," he continued, without morose. "I have no more choices left...except one."

"Don't do what I think you want to do," Patrick begged. "Please talk to me."

"This cancer has dictated every day of my life for the past five years," he vented. "I mean, it went into remission, but then came back with a vengeance. I can't take the pain anymore. I can't. The cancer hurts too much, Patrick – the chemo even more."

With inches separating them, he stopped wheeling, wavering as to what steps to take next. Patrick only knew Matt's attention needed distraction. Surprisingly, he caught himself praying that a nurse would pass by the open door or look up from the patio, noticing the distraught, teetering patient.

"Please," he begged, desperately buying time, vacillating between staying put or moving closer.

"You have a choice to make, too," Matt said, now sounding vindictive, avoiding his eyes.

"Huh?" Patrick asked, more confused.

"Can you live with yourself using that wheelchair for the rest of your life?" he challenged almost contemptuously. "Can you, Patrick? Can you?"

Patrick froze, stumped by the unexpected question. Because his world was spinning out of control, digesting the inquiry needed to wait. Matt, knowing he had momentarily distracted the remaining hurdle, looked at Patrick one last time with a knowing smile, leaned over the railing, pitching himself backwards off the balcony.

Patrick screamed, lunging to the suicidal roommate. Crashing his wheelchair into the porches red brick wall, he luckily seized one of Matt's ankles.

"Let me go, Patrick," he yelled, once realizing his friend had grabbed hold of him. "Let me go."

He thrashed about, desperately trying to free himself from the grip. The wall impact caused Patrick to slowly slide out of the wheelchair each time Matt kicked at his arm with the free leg.

"Please," Patrick wailed at no one in particular, but Matt was feeling like an anvil. "God, don't let me fall out of this chair. Don't let me fall. Don't let me fail."

Matt's weight and unrelenting fight was having the desired effect. Patrick, knowing in moments he would be thrown from the chair, felt the ankle loosening. Sensing the likely outcome, he became more distressed.

"Patrick," he insanely screamed. "Let go. It's my choice. It's mine. Make your own. Make your own fucking choice."

Already predicting the outcome, his backside began faltering on the edge of the seat. Using a forearm, he braced against the porch wall seconds before the chair flipped over, spilling him to the dusty deck floor, freeing Matt.

"Thank you," Matt's last words, trailed off, happily feeling warm, humid air whoosh around a pain-free body.

Hearing the loud thud of Matt hitting the patio floor below brought images of him looking like a gargoyle, Patrick stared blankly at his wheelchair on its side, the upper back tire systematically spinning, like a Ferris wheel at a county fair.

§§§§

Feeling sluggish, Patrick sat alone watching *Speed Racer* with the volume turned off, while Pearl rested in bed, absently tossing the infuriatingly, ever-present Nerf up in the air. Wearing dark blue, tight designer jeans, a red silk shirt and brown alligator loafers, Tony was dressed to kill – and to leave. Pete put the last of his friend's belongings in a large Gucci suitcase. Although 99X softly played in the background, not a word was exchanged between the occupants.

At the far end of the room, Sister Margaret assisted Matt's mourning parents, who wore matching linen pants and peach-colored polo shirts with a stitched-in design of their Hampton yacht club, as they finished packing their son's possessions. After zipping the last of the bags shut, the weary parents tautly headed for the door until Patrick cut them off.

"Mr. and Mrs. Clark," he started to say.

Patrick wheeled over to the box of albums and T-shirts still on the windowsill, reached in, pulling out one of each.

"These belonged to Matt," he offered.

"Thank, thank you," Mr. Clark said numbly, taking the gifts, obviously raw and confused to the finality of the recent tragedy.

"They don't look so good," Pearl prescribed, watching them leave with the nun.

"No shit," Patrick said, sounding annoyed.

"All I'm sayin' is it's gotta be tough," he responded, defensively.

"No shit," Tony chimed in, sounding even less patient.

Pete lifted the Gucci suitcase, doing a shout-out to Patrick. "Nice meetin' ya, Patrick," he said, exiting.

"Pearl and I get out tomorrow," he informed him, the words having little impact on the departing brut.

"Pete's an ignoramus," Tony said, attempting to explain. "Whattaya think he knows 'bout blacks and whites hangin', ya know?"

Tony leaned down, hugging Patrick good-bye. Pearl, losing interest in the tossing, joined their embrace.

"You gonna be cool?" Pearl asked Tony during the genuine show of affection.

"Ya know, it's been a wild week," he answered, starting to choke up. "I love yous guys."

Breaking away, Tony looked out the window, secretly wiping away a single tear. There was a distracting knock at the door, as Father Burke slowly entered the room.

"I apologize for missing Communion this morning," Father Burke said, speaking softly for the first time this week while suffering from unseen iconoclastic religious thoughts. "But I was summoned to the patio."

What happened just hours ago, was indefinable to Patrick. "Why did he do it?" he asked with disgust, watching the other roommates walk away in conversation, the priest planted himself on the edge of his bed.

"Patrick, my son, there is no answer," Father Burke attempted to explain, placing a wrinkled hand on Patrick's leg. "Matthew did what he thought he had to do. We have to accept his decision."

"But I was taught in Sunday school that killing yourself is a sin."

Looking at Patrick, his mind raced back to childhood, when he decided to become a priest at too young an age. The priest's thoughts drifted to the many years in the assigned pre-seminary high school, college, and his time as a seminarian when he was a pure acolyte, without any ambiguous thoughts. Since he was diagnosed, he found himself questioning his life, his role as a Catholic, a priest and being a man. Recently, Father Burke determined he knew little about the real world, real people, his flock and their daily sufferings.

Burke was the youngest of nine children, an Irish twin as a matter of fact. When he announced to his parents while in fourth grade that he wanted to become a priest, they were ecstatic and held him to that commitment. Within days, they informed family members, neighbors, parishioners, the postman, anyone who had two ears, the holy news. Honestly, before entering the Seminary, the thought of a life of celibacy frightened him, questioning his declaration. Several times he tried to discuss these fears with his proud mother and father but they seemed not to hear. Not wanting to disappoint, he decided to suck it up and at least finish the Seminary. After completing the required religious studies, he then opted to give the priesthood a few years.

But those few years morphed into several more, then even more. Before he knew it, Burke was in his early forties.

It would be sinful to admit he had desired several women who had crossed his path. When these situations occurred, Father Burke prayed to his God for guidance and strength. The priest was never certain if he received direct answers. However, he tended to find solace in the plenteous religious responsibilities. Having been assigned to St. Jude's in his third Diocese station, he found a calling comforting people who were ill or near death. The Archdiocese either sensed the calling, too, or simply forgot about him because they left Fr. Burke at the Catholic hospital for almost forty years.

Recently he began feeling lonely, though – emotionally empty. Most evenings were spent sipping Italian red wines, and nibbling on crusty French bread, while listening to B.B. King in a chestnut leather recliner – an extravagant purchase, especially in his later years. He would allow the soft hide to engulf his frame, enabling him to question his decisions – if the pronouncement he made as a child should have detoured somewhere along life's highway.

"I was taught that, too, many years ago," he said, finally. "Life is cloudy, it's not clear. Regardless what the Church says about suicide, there is no right or wrong, Patrick. God trusts us to make our own decisions. Matt made his."

Patrick started to choke back tears, looking at the priest, not yet comprehending the explanation.

"Look at me," the priest said, his voice full of sudden compassion. "You might have noticed my hands are shaking and I'm walking slower."

Patrick's nod indicated he did.

"I have ALS, Lou Gehrig's disease," he continued with acuity. "I was told ten months ago. It seems to be progressing faster than expected. My doctors have told me it's only a matter of time before I won't be able to perform my duties. But I understand and accept my destiny."

Smiling warmly and speaking softer still, Patrick had a difficult time hearing the next sentence. "I can empathize with Matt's decision," he said.

"Father, I need to tell you something," he said, pausing for several seconds, but leaning forward and motioning for him to inch closer, too.

"What is it?"

Looking around the room, he spotted Tony standing in front of the renowned mirror, obsessively combing his locks, still bantering with Pearl. Concluding he had the needed privacy, Patrick knew to proceed.

"Matt said something to me right before jumping."

"What was it?" Father Burke asked, concerned.

"He looked at me," he shared, trying to fathom what had transpired just hours ago. "Matt, he asked if I could live with spending the rest of my life using a wheelchair."

"Can you?" Father Burke wondered, not taken aback.

"I'm not certain," he said, hesitantly. "All I know is that I wasn't strong enough last night. I couldn't hold on. I tried...but...I wasn't. This week helped me realize I'm not physically strong enough to walk again, either."

"God may have taken the use of your legs from you, Patrick Flannery, but in return he has given you incredible strength," he began. "You may not appreciate it now, but be grateful for what you have. Don't be disappointed with what you don't. Try not to be so hard on yourself, and on this chair. I sense a wonderful journey is waiting for you."

"I did try," he admitted, honestly, trying to understand the priest's reasoning.

Father Burke gingerly stood on his feet, grabbing onto one of the chair's back wheels for balance. "I know you did," he said, praising, quickly glancing at Tony and Pearl, then back at Patrick. "And so does God. Repent nothing."

After blessing Patrick, he backed away. "I'll see you tomorrow morning," he said warmly.

"Now remember, I'm comin' by tonight wid some pasta and vino from my parents' restaurant," Tony announced, returning with Pearl, seeming anxious to check out.

"Alright," Pearl said. "And how about bringing us some dessert?"

"Whadda ya want?" Tony inquired.

"Gina."

"Ya should be so lucky," he countered, smiling.

Waving good-bye, Tony jogged the hallway to where Pete waited impatiently.

§§§§

Soaking in the blistering summer rays, Patrick sat by himself idly tapping his fingers on the small circular patio table. With lunchtime nearing, doctors, nurses and St. Jude staff members were beginning to populate surrounding chairs and tables. Administrators, insurance investigators and several police detectives milled and fretted about the still taped-off, blood-stained area where Matt landed, their crime equipment glinting in the sunshine.

Putting on the Walkman headset, he clicked the device on, shutting out the world. Replaying the recent tragedy, he questioned if his actions could have altered the outcome. Perhaps if something more profound had been offered or if he had been stronger, more fit, Matt would still be alive. And, God, what was behind the bizarre wheelchair question?

Patrick could sense a headache approaching like a distant thunder storm visible on a flat Kansas plain. He needed to relax, erase the suicide from his memory, but that was improbable – impossible. The images and words, he knew, would haunt him until his last breath. Why did he have to see or experience the inexplicable death? With eyes closed, he tried concentrating on the warmth of the sun. However, a startling shadowy presence caused him to remove the headset.

"You'll have to move this wheelchair or I'm going to give you a ticket," a familiar voice said, as Patrick squinted in a fruitless attempt to recognize the speaker's silhouette.

"Your license, please," the voice continued.

"Derrick," he said, finally putting a face to the voice, straining to be polite. Wanting no company, Patrick realized the patio was a poor selection around noon.

"You okay?" he asked, now in a hushed tone, his long work sleeves rolled up in the muggy weather.

"Hope you're not pregnant," Patrick remarked, pointing at the stacked tray of what looked to be one of everything offered on the cafeteria menu, but clearly avoiding the question.

"Nope," Derrick said, embarrassingly, caught off guard. "I lost betting against the Mets and owe the other PTs lunch."

Derrick glanced at the taped-off area, then back at Patrick. "I'm, I'm sorry about your roommate, you know," Derrick offered, haltingly.

Patrick's non-response caused Derrick to feel increasingly awkward, wanting now to make a speedy exit. He was a PT, not an emotional therapist he thought. Having fond affections for his long-time patient, he struggled to find words, which failed him.

"Man, I gotta get outta this heat," his PT finally said, leaving.

Derrick walked away but was quickly replaced by Brian, rolling in from the opposite direction. Patrick had to concede any chance of being left alone. Brian, with little success, attempted to wheel and lick an increasingly melting soft vanilla ice cream cone, simultaneously. Already, too much of the dripping treat found its way on his faded blue jeans, rather than the intended mouth. Brian tried wiping away the tiny specks of sprinkles he mistakenly added to the order off his lap.

"Gotta napkin?" he asked Patrick, somberly.

After receiving a negative response, Brian noticed an attractive medical student sitting alone at a corner table absently tossing cold, hard French Fries to pestering city pigeons.

"Think she does?" he inquired without much thought, hoping Patrick might have some insight or gossip on the young beauty.

"I don't know," he answered, matter-of-factly.

"How are you?"

"I'm fine," Patrick said, dryly.

"Really?"

"I...I'll be fine," he replied, automatically, pushing off the table, to wheel away, but stopped.

"Brian, why do you use a wheelchair?" he continued, remembering the question he kept meaning to ask since the day they were introduced.

"I did a stupid thing one night," he began, nonplussed by the inquiry, still trying to conquer the near liquid sweet. "I was a sophomore in college, hanging with a bunch of friends in my dorm, smoking a joint. We were really not partying, just hanging. Well anyway, I was sitting on the windowsill, with the window open. I was too relaxed, leaned a little too far back, lost my balance and fell out. My fall was not that much different than Matt's except it was an accident. I fell two stories and landed on grass, but still injured my spinal cord. Actions and consequences, man. That's what life is all about."

Patrick was surprised at the blunt, honest response. Drugs had never been on his radar screen. He knew, many of his classmates smoked marijuana, in fact, he was passed joints at most parties, but inhaling any type of smoke, even cigarettes, was never appealing to him. Always declining, he decided his lungs would only experience second-hand fumes during this lifetime. Brian's announcement was somewhat shocking because he never equated pot with someone other than kids he knew in high school.

"Thanks for sharing with me, Bri," Patrick said after reflecting, not certain if Brian wanted to continue.

"Hey, I've had a good life," Brian continued. "Look at me. I work, date, have a great apartment, and drive a car. There is nothing I can't do. It will be the same for you, too."

"You think so?"

They both watched a police photographer take countless photos of the precise spot where Matt landed. "No," Brian responded, with no definitive basis for the opinion. "I know so."

It was time for Patrick to leave, and he began to wheel away without saying good-bye. The courtyard, now at near capacity, strained his ability to navigate the wheelchair through and around the starved masses.

"Wait," Brian said, calling out. "I almost forgot to give you this."

Tossing the cone remains into an abandoned, lipstick-stained, empty Styrofoam cup, Brian chased him down, handing over a small cardboard box.

"I'll see you later at the pool?" he continued, smiling wanly.

"No, I'm going home tomorrow," Patrick pointed out, trying to speed the conversation up. "Gotta pack. Thanks for everything."

Brian watched him go as the dairy product remains rapidly dried on both hands. He knew they needed immediate scrubbing or that nauseating smell of sour milk would permeate into his skin. Turning, he saw a pack of pigeons pecking away at the remaining fries on the departed medical student's paper plate.

§§§§

The two remaining roommates rested in their respective beds, staring at Tony and Matt's stripped-bare space. Pearl nervously fidgeted, anally playing with the ever-present Nerf basketball. Patrick stared at a framed picture of two people in a small boat, rowing on a lake with a setting sun. This inexpensive print, mounted on the wall directly across from his bed, had been present since the first time he was assigned the room. However, for the first time, he noticed a swan swimming directly behind the boat. How could he have ever missed the animal before, he wondered? Was he that dense?

"Yo, homes, dinner better be gettin' here soon," Pearl remarked. "I'm hungry."

"Tony said he's bringing his mom's pasta," Patrick replied.

"When, man, when?"

"Soon," he said to his roommate. "Don't worry, he'll be here."

Pearl threw the Nerf ball toward Patrick, who caught it, quickly pitching it back. Something had been bothering him about Pearl but with each passing day, he had less courage to inquire. No one had visited the guy the entire time they had shared the room. In fact, Patrick realized his roommate never mentioned family members or friends. Although feeling uncomfortable broaching the subject, Patrick decided this was the first, and perhaps, only opportune time.

"Pearl," he announced. "How come no one has come to see you this week?"

Not missing a beat, he bounced the ball off the ceiling. "Maybe it's because I ain't got no people who wants to come visit," he said, bluntly.

For a moment, Patrick looked at this mysterious, artistically gifted roommate, digesting the delivered simplistic logic. Pearl, changed bouncing directions and began hurling the mini b-ball against the farthest wall.

"But you haven't had friends visit either."

"Patrick, you are askin' me need-to-know questions," he said, testily, stopping his tossing activity. "And as far as I'm concerned, you ain't needin' to know the answers."

That concluded this particular conversation, but it only heightened Patrick's natural curiosity. It amazed him he had no idea who Pearl really was, where he was from, or where he would go after being discharged. Not looking to pick a fight, Patrick turned his attention to Brian's box, which lay on his bedstand. Out of curiosity, he finally opened it, pulling out a small bottle of clear fluid, instantly attracting Pearl's attention.

"Whatcha got?"

"I'm not sure," Patrick honestly said, reading the instruction label. "Hey, it's Papaverin."

"Papraven?" Pearl countered, having difficulty pronouncing the word, earnestly observing his roommate holding a thin, plastic, unused syringe up in the air.

"Hey," Pearl went on, excitingly. "Alright."

"What?" Patrick asked, clueless to what he said.

Patrick read the small print descriptive directions, unsuccessfully trying to fill the syringe with the drug. Frustrated, he crumpled the thin paper, tossing it in the direction of the nearest refuge pail.

"This one is different," he informed, quickly, still experimenting.

Patrick awkwardly refilled, tapped the syringe, trying to clear it of various sized air bubbles. Frowning, he squeezed to release a bit of fluid, but instead, pushed too hard, completely emptying the tube like a high-pressured water pistol.

"Damn," Patrick said, embarrassingly.

Pearl, tired of watching waste, and wanting to display his proficiency, hobbled over. "Yo," he said stopping Patrick. "Hold it, man. Let me do that."

Like a seasoned physician, Pearl, cleaned the top of the bottle with the provided alcohol pad, taking off the cap of an enclosed fresh needle. While turning the bottle upside down, he deftly inserted, withdrawing the clear liquid. After extracting, he tapped the syringe twice, forcing remaining air pockets to the top, gently squeezed the syringe executing a successful trickle test. He then succinctly recapped the needle, handing the finished product to his anxiously waiting friend.

"What's this stuff for?" he asked Patrick, shaking the remaining medicine in the bottle.

"Nothing special," he replied, impressed with another previously unknown Pearl expertise.

"You've shot up before?"

"No," he admitted.

"Oh, shit," Pearl said, placing the bottle on Patrick's bed.

"It's okay," he offered. "I'll hardly feel it."

"Whattaya mean?" he asked. "Come on, man, get real. Look, I've done this before."

"When?"

Pearl inadvertently revealed more than he meant to. "Uh, for my sick grandmother," he said, picking up the full syringe, deflecting. "So let me help you."

He started investigating for a waiting vein in Patrick's wounded right arm. The past week's blood-taking expeditions left few viable options. After locating an inviting location, Pearl opened up another alcohol package to disinfect the skin.

"No, no, wait," Patrick said, in an attempt to educate.

"It's not for the arm."

"Oh, okay," Pearl said, a bit bewildered. "Where then? Your shoulder?"

Patrick nodded "no".

"Your leg?" he guessed again.

Another "no" nod.

"Your wrist?" he continued speculating, running out of bodily locations. "Behind your ear?"

"Here," he said, pointing between his legs.

"There?" the roommate said standing up. "Serious? No way"

He handed Pearl the remaining enclosed instructional pictograms, his black skin paling after confirming. Dropping the renderings, he hopped back to his bed.

"Serious."

"Homie, you is on your own."

Patrick pulled up the bedsheet, covering his lower extremities. Sliding the sweat pants down, he propped his legs, used one of the unopened alcohol pads to thoroughly clean his penis and surrounding skin.

"I'm outta here," Pearl said after watching him pick-up the fluid-filled cylinder.

Grabbing the crutches, he hobbled out. Patrick was now alone. Squeamishly, he injected the medicine as the radio ran a "Raceway Park" commercial. The Papaverin entered his body, a trickle of blood visible in the clear cylinder. Patrick removed the needle, inspecting the punctured area. Capping the soiled medical device, he ripped opened the last of the alcohol pads, applying pressure to the puncture.

"Noooo," Pearl cried out from the doorway, reentering the room a bit too early.

With a sly smile evident, Patrick looked at the woozy roommate leaning against the door, whose hands covered his own private parts.

"You is crazy," Pearl said. "Cra-zy."

Patrick threw the used pads away when Gregory, a loud yellow scarf draping his neck, glided in carrying two dinner trays at an inopportune moment.

"Get that crap out of here, Mr. Gregory," the injected roomie directed, scornfully. "Real food's coming."

"Well, excuse me," he said, sounding personally insulted, as he retreated.

"Man, don't be turnin' away good food like that," Pearl complained.

"Who needs it?" he asked. "Our pasta man is coming any minute."

Patrick inspected his body, stunned to see his bed sheet shaped like a pup tent. Smiling, he was already sprouting.

"Lemme try some of that shit," Pearl joked, observing the covered projectile.

Their private viewing session was interrupted by the loud telephone ringing. Patrick, thinking it was Tony calling with an arrival update, lunged for the phone.

"Hey, shithead, get Gina over here quick," Patrick shouted. "I'm ready...Oh, hi, Mom...No, no, no, it's just a gag...I'm sorry...What?...You heard about my roommate?...Could we talk about it when you and Dad pick me up?...Huh, Dad's mad?...I know, about the other day...I know you do...and I love you, Mom...

Half-listening, Patrick could not help but lift up the sheet for a quick inspection. Feeling proud with the pronounced erection, a guilt-ridden thought occurred to him that somehow his mother possessed powers enabling her to see through phone lines.

"Mom, I gotta go," he said, hurrying to end their awkward conversation. "No problem, but I gotta go...No, everything is fine. See you tomorrow...Love you, too."

Slamming down the phone in horror, his roommate already howled hysterically. Terror-stricken, Patrick eventually joined in.

"It's the drug," Patrick said, defensively. "Oh my God. I'm going to hell."

The two friends continued laughing when Patrick's clock read 5:45 pm.

§§§§

"Patrick?" Mrs. Flannery spoke.

She hung up the kitchen wall-mounted phone, while Dana stood nearby pouring Diet Coke into a tall ice-filled glass given to them this afternoon by a local gas station for filling up their car with premium gas. She watched her mother, who appeared bewildered, open the oven, peering in on a roasting chicken surrounded by peeled potatoes and searing carrots.

"What's up with my big bro?" Dana asked, helping arrange the table for dinner.

"You know, I'm not sure," Mrs. Flannery replied, honestly.

Feeling old, she sat at the table, ignoring Dana placing the utensils at the three place settings. After finishing, she sat with her mother, helping as they both briskly husked ears of corn. Mrs. Flannery wore a sweater because the recently installed central conditioner pushed down frigid air from ceiling-mounted air ducts.

Most, if not all, of her classmates had contentious teenage relationships with their respective mothers, but Dana considered her mom to be a close friend, a confidant, in fact. They liked to take shopping excursions, attend Broadway plays or movies, and even garden together. She suspected there was an ever-present void in her mother's life, however. Most relatives and friends viewed Jack as the leader of the family, but Dana knew better. Her mother was the glue, the true Rock of Gibraltar. She kept it all together through the rough and stormy times. Whenever situations permitted, Mrs. Flannery ended sentences with, "God is good."

Dana could not remember Patrick's accident, but she was old enough to remember how certain dynamics, a few financial, but mostly emotional, changed following the tragedy. At times, her mom needed nothing more than someone to listen, and Dana did her best, even when too young, to be that sounding board.

"Have you spoken with Dr. Goodman this week?" Dana asked, pressing before placing a finished cob into a Tupperware bowl placed between them on the hardwood floor.

Mrs. Flannery glanced out the back of the patio French doors, watching her husband finish mowing their mostly scorched backyard grass, before rising to check an enormous metal pot with near surging, boiling water resting on a red-hot back burner. She washed the fresh corn but said nothing, a vague look on her face.

"Did Dr. Goodman call?" Dana asked again, placing the cobs one-by-one into the ready water after Mrs. Flannery finished rinsing.

"Mom?" Dana repeated again, covering the pot, steam immediately emanating from the seams.

"Mom?"

Startled, she twirled, hearing Dana for the first time, who approached with a long embrace. Mrs. Flannery felt her body melt in the affection.

"I feel like everything is getting so out of control," she confessed.

"Talk to me," she said, releasing her mother. "What's wrong?"

Pulling away, she kissed her mature beyond years daughter's forehead, and sat again at the kitchen table. "Oh, my love," she started, her voice trembling.

"What?" the younger one replied, genuinely concerned.

Dana raced back to lower the oven burner temperature where the overflowing scalding water was practically blowing off the slightly dented stainless steel pot cover.

"I feel so helpless."

"Helpless?" Dana asked, now turning down the burner before jumping onto the bright white Formica counter. "What do you mean?"

"Dr. Goodman did phone this afternoon and, needless to say, the news was not encouraging," she volunteered. "He told me things did not work out again with your brother and the braces."

Dana looked shocked, rolling her eyes. "Wow," she said. "I really thought this year…Does dad know?"

"No he doesn't," Mrs. Flannery confided. "I'm not sure how to tell him."

"How is Patrick?" Dana naturally wondered. "Is he ok?"

Mrs. Flannery pointed to padded pot holding gloves resting next to the sink. Dana obediently put them on before removing the ready roasting chicken from the stove.

"I think your brother will handle things well," she said, truthfully.

"I think so, too," Dana answered, resting the hissing cooked chicken on the table center.

She looked directly at Dana. "It's your father I worry about," she confided, bleakly.

Moments passed, before their silence was interrupted by the house doorbell.

"It's probably the paper boy, collecting for the month," Mrs. Flannery guessed. "I left his money on the coffee table."

Dana walked into the living room feeling guilty for not appropriately comforting her loving mother. Finding the money in the instructed location, Dana went to open the front door seconds after it rang again.

§§§§

Mrs. Flannery sat at the kitchen table, playing with a fork, deep in thought. Ordinarily, she ignored the raucous music originating from her son's bedroom.

It was not unusual for Patrick to continually repeat a favorite song, allowing her the opportunity to focus and memorize the lyrics. Lately, he began playing a particular track over and over again. Though she eventually grew weary of the tune, the words jumped out, especially the first verse, now engrained in her mind.

"And you may find yourself living in a shotgun shack…And you may find yourself in another part of the world…And you may find yourself behind the wheel of a large automobile…And you may find yourself in a beautiful house, with a beautiful wife, and you may ask yourself-well…how did I get here?"'

Just yesterday afternoon, while alone at home, Mrs. Flannery found the album still on Patrick's turntable. After several trial and errors, she proudly mastered the endless control buttons, cued the song, sat on her son's neatly made bed and allowed the lyrics to flow.

Mrs. Flannery thought herself to be a practical person. How did she get here, she reflected? Yes, her life seemed almost too perfect to outside observers, but Patrick's accident changed that forever. Everyone was fallible, but was God punishing them, or her specifically, for unknown sins?

Feeling chilled in the crisp room, Mrs. Flannery rubbed her shivering arms, then dabbed at her eyes with a folded, cloth table napkin.

§§§§

Three hours later, Patrick was still horizontal in bed, watching his still-erect penis, droplets of sweat increased their path down a now flush face. The initial amazement over the injection had drifted to concern. Nervously, he reread the drug's instructions, speculating he made a dosage error, but the damn Nerf smacked him right between the eyes.

"That's the longest erection I've ever seen," Pearl pestered. "When's it coming down?"

"About an hour ago."

Pearl glanced at the empty syringe. "While you're still hard, I'm still hungry," he said, his voice edgy. "Where's that Italian?"

Patrick knew his roommate had a ravenous appetite. He would eat anything, anytime. Appeasing Pearl, he picked up the phone, dialing Tony's number.

"You know, it's Friday night, his folks' restaurant is probably swamped," he said more to himself.

Before Pearl could reply, the opposite end answered the call on the first ring. "Hi, Pete?" Patrick guessed. "This is Patrick. Yeah, Tony's hospital roommate. I, I can hardly hear you. Is Tony there?"

"Sounds like a party," he went on louder, watching Pearl, who, acting as if he had already heard enough, reached for one more Devil Dog. "Tony? When you coming over?"

§§§§

Tony's cubed backyard was flush with catered food platters and jammed with neighborhood young people. Most stood, some danced in the tight space, serviced by a lone porch light and temporarily hung tropical lanterns. Although a vast majority of the males were well-built, they paled in comparison to Pete. Madonna's "Holiday" blared in the smoky exterior environment, the guests drinking mixed fruity drinks.

"Whaddya mean," Tony said casually annoyed, cupping the phone to drown out the back noise. "I'm right here. Where do ya think I am?"

"You said you were coming over," Patrick said, already feeling uncomfortable.

Tony gestured to Pete for the stereo to be turned down. "Who, who da fuck is dis?" Tony shouted.

"It's me, Patrick," he replied.

Lightning struck. Tony had allowed himself to be completely distracted by the improvised festivities. In retrospect, gone for only a week, he was not the least bit shocked his boys wanted to celebrate. But he had clearly forgotten about visiting his new-found friends with the promised food.

"Buddy, how da hell are ya?" he asked, doing his best to stall.

"You said…" Patrick started to say.

"Hey, I rememba what I said, gimme a break," Tony said sourly, cutting him off. "But my family, ya know, wanted to throw me dis big party and I can't get out just yet. All my aunts, uncles and cousins are here, ya know?"

Gina walked by, abruptly thrusting her tongue in his ear. Disgusted, Tony pushed her away, a little too roughly.

Patrick backed off. "Sorry for calling," he said.

"Look, I'll come by as soon as my relatives leave," Tony said, arrogantly, clearly trying to fob off his former roommate. "Okay?"

Gina, not to be discouraged, began kissing and biting his neck, whispering. "Ya better cum," she said.

"Listen, forget about it," Patrick said uneasily, recognizing the female voice in the background. "Pearl and I will be fine."

Tony shoved Gina, forcing her onto Pete's lap. "Hey, don't be actin' like no fag, ya know?" the contrarian said into the headset. "I said I'm coming. I'll see ya when I get there."

"Good night," Patrick responded only to himself, hanging up, looking again at his still fully sprouted penis.

§§§§

Patrick wished he could have been surprised by Tony's change of colors, but who was he kidding? He had never kept in touch with past hospital mates…and there had been too many already. Secretly, he hoped this week's events would have made the current relationships different. But being wrong, again, saddened him. Looking at Pearl, he was overcome by a foreboding that this was, in all likelihood, their last evening together.

§§§§

Pearl finished a third borrowed Devil Dog, scarfing while lying in bed with his security blanket substitute…the Nerf ball. Patrick, set his radio's volume to maximum decibel levels, pulled the bed sheet over his head, enabling him to stare at his ever-present erect penis, frightened.

His calculating roommate slipped out of bed, quietly invading Patrick's nightstand with atypical avidity. Reaching into the top open drawer, he absconded an unused needle and syringe. Closing his bed curtain, he pulled a packet of heroin from the hiding place, laying it neatly on the sheets. The habit got the best of him, once again.

§§§§

The clock read 9:05 when Pearl, consumed with such restlessness, jumped over to Patrick's bed, pulling away the sheet from Patrick's head.

"Come on, P-man," he shouted, restive. "We're takin' a walk."

"Now?"

"This room is makin' me insane," he replied, his demeanor somewhat anxious. "Let's go."

Pearl was flying like a kite, in a fictive state. The purchased street drugs were of higher quality than he was accustomed. Usually, the potency was drastically reduced, having been cut with each passing hand.

But this stash was quite pure. Also, having been clean for sometime, his body was reacting as it had the first time he injected. This rush was climatic. Already clutching one of his crutches, he initiated rhythmic knocking against Patrick's bedstand, the pace quickening expeditiously.

"Come on, come on," he continued, chanting interminably.

Patrick gingerly transferred to his wheelchair, trying not to damage his revived organ. More and more, he thought a call to Brian might be prudent.

"Look at this," he pleaded. "I can't go anywhere."

"You're covered," Pearl said, flinging a wash towel over his roommate's lap, exiting before Patrick could protest or properly adjust the towel.

§§§§

The pair waited for an elevator, one patiently, the other not so. In due course, one arrived, and in a flash, Pearl, babbling about a fictional game of one-on-one, entered, Patrick right behind. However, a firm hand appeared out of thin air, grabbed his arm, stopping his wheelchair in mid-stride. Stunned, he glanced back only to discover Mary and Sister Margaret standing together, the nun not letting go of her prized catch. He could not recall any recent transgressions that would have put him, or them, in hot water with the obviously perturbed floor warden.

"And where do you think you two boys are going?" Sister Margaret said, her voice thundering.

Turning his chair to face the women, words failed him. Patrick was not certain if he detected anger or disappointment, perhaps both.

"Just to the patio, Sis," Pearl answered innocently, stopping his invisible basketball contest.

"And what mischief might we be hiding under here, Patrick Flannery?" Sister Margaret inquired, eying the two with deep suspicion, expecting a palpable lie.

Without hesitation, she whipped the towel off, exposing Patrick's pup tent. Having expected a hidden bottle of some type of alcohol, she was ill-prepared for the discovery.

"Jesus, Mary and Joseph," she prayed, nearly fainting. "Jesus, Mary and Joseph."

Dropping the cloth, she scurried off, most likely to the hospital chapel, repeatedly making the sign of the cross with one hand, holding her rosaries with the other, reciting a prayer of Expiation.

"Why, Mr. Patrick, I see someone here is not suffering from the Irish curse," Mary observed, smiling, tucking in the towel under his legs concealing his largeness. "Pity for me."

Embarrassed, Patrick backed into the elevator, giving the nurse a meek wave before the doors finally closed.

§§§§

The vast patio sat empty when Patrick and Pearl entered this late hour. On the far side, a middle-aged, Hispanic man, strangely wearing sunglasses in the dimly lit area, emptied rectangular garbage pails with the ever increasingly present hospital insignia painted on all four sides, into a large dark green dumpster he lugged around. The evening's air still sizzled with little breeze to offer comfort.

Pearl, allowing the drugs to take him elsewhere, wandered off singing the lyrics to "Amazing Grace," while looking aimlessly up at the adjoining hospital buildings. Patrick wheeled over to the section of patio where Matt landed.

He kind of gawked at the taped body outline on the patio floor. After several moments, he wheeled away, nearing Pearl, who continued singing but now from a patio table acting as a temporary stage. For no apparent reason, he lifted his towel to discover his pup tent had vanished.

"Yo," he said, calling excitingly out to Pearl. "I don't have an erection. I lost the erection."

Glancing over, the cleaning man could not tell who he should be more wary about, the reckless kid singing on the table or the peculiar gringo exclaiming something about his penis. Just wanting to complete his nightly job responsibilities, he surmised they had wandered off the psychiatric floor. Clearly nonplussed, the man had a notion to notify his supervisor, but that would require some effort, and only on summer nights was he unwilling to work overtime, knowing frosty beers awaited on his apartment's front stoop. Deciding their offenses to be minor, he decided keeping silent would hasten his departure.

"My Man ain't got no e-REC-tion," he comically whooped, frequently babbling to the unseen Gods, embracing the euphoria engulfing his every pore. "My man got no e-rec-TION."

Pearl continued to loudly ramble, lost in another world. Looking around the enclosure, Patrick noted the cleaning man had departed.

"Pearl, could we keep the erection thing to ourselves?" Patrick whispered.

Pearl then repeated the request, only much louder. "Keep the E-rec-TION thing to ourselves," he said, not realizing the ingested narcotic had taken control. "Keep the E-REC-TION thing to ourselves."

Frequently accustomed to Pearl's quirkiness, Patrick sensed the endless recitation meant he was not well. Intuit by nature, he attempted to calm and return him back to their room as quickly as possible after detecting dilated eyes and minor foaming at the mouth corners.

"Come on, Pearl," he said, a little too bluntly, acting as caretaker. "It's getting late. Let's go back upstairs."

Pearl continued loudly repeating every word spoken by Patrick, but became unnervingly silent after descending the table, erratically walking parallel with his companion.

§§§§

Finally safe in an empty elevator, Patrick pressed the tenth floor button, his concern increasing for the roommate's bizarre, uneven behavior. Mere minutes from reaching their room, he was feeling less comfortable with the immediate quagmire now facing him. Pearl kept whimpering incoherently, while Patrick vainly attempted to assuage him, the creaky box slowly climbing the building.

"It's okay, Pearl," he said, reassuringly, but frightened. "It's okay, buddy. We are almost home."

Without warning, the drug-induced patient gradually slid, slumping to the floor, mumbling what sounded like an incantation. Pearl's deteriorating physical and mental states only heightened Patrick's worries, who anxiously watched the call buttons, audibly counting the passing hospital floors.

"Come on," he urged, speculating this situation would only worsen. "Get moving, you piece of shit machine."

In that instance, the elevator came to a crashing stop, causing Pearl to convulse and nearly throwing Patrick out of his wheelchair. Disoriented, he regained his balance, before grasping the fact they were stuck several feet beneath the seventh floor.

"Relax," he said more to himself, inspecting the thrashing roommate, trying not to sound alarmed, but feeling a foreboding that Pearl's condition would continue worsening with each passing second. "Help is on the way."

But he knew Pearl could not hear the fib. Confused, Patrick felt himself panicking, hitting every button on the wall control call panel. Frightened, he resorted to punching the doors when the elevator failed to respond.

Wishing for his parents' presence – they would surely know what needed to be done to help Pearl – Patrick took a deep breath and forced himself to calm down before noticing an emergency phone door on the lower corner panel. Opening it, his heart sank after discovering a single wire, the exposed end connected to air. Pearl's thrashing advanced to a full-fledged seizure, spittle oozing from his open mouth.

"Help," he yelled, banging on the elevator doors contemptuously. "Can anyone hear? We're stuck on the seventh floor. Help."

Sensing his screams fell only on deaf ears, and fearful Pearl might bite off his tongue, he remembered a movie shown in last year's health class describing epilepsy. Recalling a particular scene, he removed a slipper, jamming it into the lashing roommate's mouth. He knew it was time to gain some semblance of control, if not, Pearl would surely die and two deaths in one week were beyond anyone's quota. Patrick could almost hear his father giving his simple instructions: "You're alone. Pearl needs help, so deal with it."

"It's okay," he said, frightfully, but assuringly. "I'll get us out."

Turning, he pried open the interior elevator doors a few inches. As suspected, Patrick discovered the cab sat two feet beneath the floor. Without hesitating, he parallel parked his wheelchair against the doors, engaged its brakes lifting his backside onto an armrest. He then attempted to open the exterior doors, but they were slightly out of reach for proper leverage.

No matter how much he strained, the interior doors would barely budge. Through the tiny crack, Patrick detected the floor was dimly lit, and probably unoccupied.

"Damn, it's the operating floor," he muttered to himself, remembering. "No one is going to be there at this time."

He looked back and forth at his wheelchair and Pearl, already knowing what needed to be done. Fears, which only moments ago had overwhelmed him, had dissipated. Patrick was regaining composure.

"Don't let me down chair," he said, calmly speaking to it like a pal. "Please don't let me down. I need you."

Still sitting precariously on the armrest, Patrick gritted his teeth, reached over, pulling out the other armrest from its socket. Trying one final time, he gallantly opened the shut doors, scarcely enough to wedge the armrest through the tight opened space. Now using the armrest as a lever, he somehow disengaged the locking mechanism after struggling moments, opening the doors completely.

"Come on, chair," he said, looking down at both Pearl and his wheelchair. "Come on."

With one graceful motion, Patrick seized a wheelchair push handle, hoisting himself up onto the faintly lighted operating hallway floor. His hunch was correct; no one appeared to be in the vicinity. Spotting a telephone perched on a nearby desk, he crawled, dragging his bruised and battered body along the cool floor toward the phone.

"Thank you, wheelchair," he said, crying unexpectedly. "Thank you, God."

Reaching the tall metal desk, Patrick pulled hard on the dangling cord, too hard, causing it to crash to the solid floor, shattering upon impact. Devastated, defeat seemed imminent.

"Hey, you," a voice unexpectedly called out from the other end of the long, darken corridor. "You on the floor. What the hell are you doing up here?"

Patrick rolled over to face the unrecognizable approaching figure. Because of the dimness, it took several seconds before he distinguished it to be the same young, unctuous Dr. Martin, who initially dawdled, then quickened his pace the closer he came.

"Help me," he choked, only able to point. "I think my roommate's dying."

"Oh, my God," Dr. Martin exclaimed, after peering inside.

The doctor scampered by Patrick, pushed a prominent red circular wall button, activating a hospital-wide alarm and intercom system. Dr. Martin ripped off the white staff coat, while expertly barking orders.

"This is Dr. Martin," he shouted into the intercom. "I've got a Code on the seventh floor."

The doctor returned to the elevator, squeezed through the opening, only to disappear into the illuminating cab. Suspicious, Patrick scooted after him, peering in to catch a glimpse as Dr. Martin checked Pearl's vitals. His roommate's complexion had turned a peculiar black.

Within minutes, hospital staff, including Benny, arrived to the seventh floor from all directions, some using rarely accessed stairwells. Most raced past Patrick, some with medical machinery, to join the young doctor.

"Please help him," Patrick said to no one, everyone. "He has to be alright."

A constant flow of personnel flooded the area, bedlam consumed the entire perimeter. Benny turned his attention toward Patrick, pulling him away from the scene.

"You got to save Pearl, Voo-Doo Man," he implored, something snapping emotionally. "Do you hear me?"

Benny barely nodded yes, having a difficult time with his patient, clinging to his shoulders. Dr. Goodman arrived on the floor as Patrick began struggling with several hospital staff who had only wanted to assist their co-worker.

"Patrick," his doctor barked.

He neither heard nor detected Goodman's presence in the midst of what was becoming mortal combat. Patrick attempted to return to Pearl, but too many people blocked the opening. A traumatized Dr. Martin clambered out, having been replaced by more seasoned emergency physicians. A ballistic Patrick spotted the overmatched professional, pacing nearby, roughly rubbing his hands together.

"You asshole," Patrick said, venting furiously at Dr. Martin. "You better not fuck up with him like you did with me. You hear me, you fuck? What's the matter with you? Tell me."

Dr. Martin, oblivious to the abrupt onslaught, vomited on his scrubs, without warning. Hospital brethren raced to assist as the elevator doors closed, taking Pearl and Patrick's empty wheelchair to an unknown destination.

"Where did they go?" Patrick persistently challenged, crawling away from the group, raving like a lunatic. "This is a fucking hospital. Where did they go?"

"We're helping your roommate, Mon," Benny implored, trying to calm him.

"He's not my roommate, he's my friend," Patrick cried deliriously, swelling with venom. "He's my friend. Don't you understand? You hear me? Where's my fuckin' chair? Get my chair. Where's my fucking chair?"

Patrick, the tempest, momentarily escaped the grips of the formidable opponents, finding enough space and time to scuttle over to a neighboring supply cabinet. After opening, the unrelenting patient hurled urinals, bedpans, anything he could possibly possess, with abandonment, at the direction of the nurses who only minutes ago attempted to restrain him. Ducking and dodging, an orderly finally reached Patrick.

"Patrick, stop it," Dr. Goodman ordered, racing over.

Patrick sharpened his aim. Battling the nurses and orderlies with astonishing ferocity, he eventually got the upper hand, putting Benny into a headlock.

"I'm in trouble here, people," Voo-Doo Man called out, searching for support. "This kid is stronger than a mofo."

An orderly, with a Star of David tattooed on the top of his exposed, shaved skull, tentatively approached. However, Patrick, with his remaining free arm, quickly put him into an equally tight headlock.

"Get me 5 mg of Haldol and 2 mg of Ativan," Dr. Goodman commanded to anyone within earshot.

A second orderly vainly tried loosening the grip around Benny's neck, while a diminutive resident scampered for the ordered drugs. After extreme effort, they all finally immobilized Patrick to the ground.

"Get the hell off of me you fucks," he nihilistically screamed, spittle and sweat flying in all directions.

"Move quickly," Dr. Goodman ordered, once the resident reappeared.

She apprehensively held the full syringe upright, like a policewoman preparing to subdue a suspect with a raised firearm for the first time.

"Get off me you bastards," Patrick bellowed, deliriously. "Get off me! Pearl! Pearl! Tony! Tony! Where are you? Help me, Matt! Where's my chair? Get me my wheelchair!"

"What are you doing?" Patrick continued barking, menacingly, witnessing the female resident jab him with the first tranquilizer, then with the follow-up. "Fuck you! You're trying to kill me? Fuck you...I'm not going under. You are not putting me under."

"I'll take care of him," Dr. Goodman informed the rest of the staff. "Just get me the stretcher."

"You think you are tough, big guys," he said, but speaking with difficultly, the drugs instantly having their intended effect. "Well, yuck...yuck...foo."

Patrick realized the nadir had been reached as his remaining vision fluttered before fading to black.

§§§§

Wearily, Patrick lifted his stiff, upper body off an expansive, navy blue cushioned physical therapy mat placed on the roof's surface. Still drowsy, he sighed while stretching surprisingly rigid muscles and aching arms. With a dampened mood, he surveyed the extensive visible body bruises, wondering if he had just experienced a terrible dream. But how did he get up here? A substantial memory void existed.

Edie inadvertently answered some questions simply by pushing his wheelchair next to where he rested. Patrick noted a black plastic cubed-shaped transistor radio, as well as other items positioned on the seat. The radio softly played, "Ooh Child" by Dee Dee Sharp, the New York City skyline lights illuminated in the background. He began focusing on the surroundings, then at Edie who wore torn, light blue jeans and an untucked, wrinkled, button-down white oxford.

"How long have you been awake?" she asked, kneeling down on the mat next to him.

"A few minutes," he said, speculating, rubbing his listless eyes, attempting to recollect his thoughts. "How long have I been asleep?"

"Close to four hours."

"It wasn't a dream, was it?" he asked. He did not move as she edged closer still.

"Pearl's dead," Edie finally responded. "They found a lot of heroin in his system."

"We were both supposed to leave today," Patrick said, slowly, having already sensed the outcome. Total exhaustion engulfed his body, forcing him back to a prone position on the mat.

"Dr. Goodman called your parents after the ordeal," she continued. "They're still planning to pick you up in the morning."

"Why? Why are you...," he inquired without completing his thought, as he noted her nervously playing with the radio's volume.

"Brian called and told me what happened," she said, proceeding to inch nearer. "I had Derrick carry you up. They tell me you gave them quite a workout. You tired everyone out. So I'm here in relief."

"Thanks," he said, again opening his eyes.

Soothed merely by her presence, neither spoke for what seemed like several minutes. They eavesdropped on the background sounds emanating from the streets below. Edie eventually rested her head so they shared the sole pillow.

For unknown reasons, even to him, Patrick decided to change the subject. "When I had my accident I was playing baseball," he said. "I was only seven."

"Excuse me?"

"I was playing centerfield in a Little League game," he spoke blithely. "My dad was watching. Mike Hopper was at the plate when I heard the noise. I turned and out of nowhere came this big, old blue Chevy. It swerved off the road, crashed through the fence, and onto the field where we were playing; where I was standing. It was coming right at me."

"Are you sure you want to talk about this?" she asked hesitantly, readjusting the pillow under their heads.

He continued the trance-like dialogue. "The driver was drunk, you know," he said, as she politely nodded.

"I jumped out of the way," Patrick said, grimly. "Thought I made it, too, but I turned around and saw my left foot get caught under the wheel. It threw me thirty-five feet. The impact broke my hip and left leg, and injured my spine. The rest is history."

Edie listened compassionately, brushing the ruffled hair from his forehead. She was charmed by both the honesty and strength.

"What happened to the driver?"

"Nothing," he said, finally. "The guy is still driving. He hit me when DWI laws were almost non-existent. We sued and settled out of court. I hear he's living in Florida."

"Are you going to be alright?" she wondered.

"My accident was on August 4th," he admitted, almost nonchalantly. "I remember on the seventh anniversary of being hit. It was just over three years ago. It was a benchmark because it meant I had spent more time in my life using a wheelchair than having walked. Without my parents knowing, I went to my bedroom and bawled like a baby. That's when I came to the realization that being a paraplegic might be a lifelong engagement."

Edie sat up, beginning to remove food from a brown grocery bag. "You hungry?" she asked, at a loss for the appropriate response. "I know you haven't eaten all day."

Patrick smiled for the first time but shook his head no. He watched as she slid next to him again, their faces mere inches apart.

"I broke up with Todd," Edie said, changing the subject.

"Huh?" he stammered, his eyes widened.

"I'm not ready to marry."

"Really?" he asked, surprised.

"Yes."

Patrick spoke not a word, instead he continued looking at Edie, feeling her warm breath. Strangely, the sensation had a calming effect.

"So what are you going to do?"

"I'm workin' on it," she countered, not worried of her changed matrimonial future.

"Why are you telling me?" he inquired, needing to know.

"I guess because you're my friend" she answered.

"Well, my friend, I know I'm not going to ever walk again," he said, shifting the flow of the conversation.

"Are you okay with that?" she replied, with evident concern.

"Yeah, I am," Patrick said, grateful to finally articulate the pent-up feeling. "Both my wheelchair and I are okay with it."

Edie looked over at his empty chair, then back at him. "Remember the last time we were on the roof?" she wondered, mischievously.

Patrick said nothing, their conversation suddenly vexing him.

"We talked about friends," she continued, her voice becoming surprisingly seductive while he looked confused.

"We talked about special friends, remember?" she went on, attempting to clarify her previous words.

Edie gingerly kissed Patrick's upper lip. "I'm that special friend," she whispered, softly tutoring.

They gazed at each other, as she lifted her head to delicately kiss both cheeks, the still wounded nose, chin, and then lips.

"I don't think I understand," Patrick said nervously, but not entirely truthful.

"I'm that friend," she blithely volunteered, tenderly kissing his lips again.

She continued kissing his lips, again and again. Patrick gradually succumbed, longing for the kisses, their lips pulsated before they separated.

"Oh, that friend," he stated, with semi-confidence.

She grinned, carefully unbuttoning her shirt. But he grabbed her hand before the last button could be undone.

"Edie, wait," he exclaimed, exasperated. "Why? I mean...why me. You could have any non-disabled guy."

"Because it's you."

"But, what if I let you down?" he said a bit tentatively. "What if I can't."

"You can only hurt me if you're into S&M," she replied, amused.

"M&M's?" he asked.

She stifled a laugh. "Patrick," Edie said, simply, slipping her hands to remove her white oxford.

"I found some Papaverin," she volunteered, picking up a small needle and syringe.

"No needles," he said, near gasping, tentatively sliding the bra straps from her shoulders. "No more needles."

She tossed the unused paraphernalia away as they continued kissing, lifting his torso off the mat to assist in deftly removing his shirt, pajama bottoms and briefs.

"Are we pretending we're in New Hampshire?" he said teasingly.

"Shut up, Patrick," she countered, amused.

He unsnapped her bra, after she eased out of her jeans, resuming their kissing, first softly, then passionately. The young virgin reached down to stimulate himself but Edie removed his hands, pinning them on the mat over his head, eventually letting go so she could stimulate his body.

"That's my job," she cooed, but assertively.

Edie gently ran her tongue around his neck, chest, and stomach, pursuing a downward trajectory. Patrick reacted to physical emotions he had yet to experience. After much time, they reached an ecstasy almost at the identical moment.

Slowly, the New York City skyline lights began to dim.

§§§§

Patrick awoke wallowing in sybaritic splendor…literally. He never expected to lose his virginity this week. In fact, he was resigned to not experience intimacy for many years, if at all. And to his utter amazement, the moment itself was picture-perfect. A romance novel might not be able to duplicate. Perhaps because it was so unexpected, or because he made love for the first time, with a friend who made him feel comfortable, confident and attractive. In the end, it did not matter. Patrick was less fearful and more self-assured about all things, especially his future.

The room was devoid of the sounds of 99x when Father Burke entered the room with Communion. "Body of Christ," he bellowed, his voice booming again in the hollow space.

"Amen," Patrick responded.

"Good-bye, Father," he said, with his mouth still full, before the priest departed.

"I'll be leaving today," Patrick continued after Burke ceased a backward shuffle.

For reasons Patrick did not comprehend, the cleric appeared astonished by the news, pausing before responding. "I'm always praying for you, Patrick," he offered generously.

"We'll see you next year," he said more asking than telling.

"I hope so," the priest said peacefully. "I honestly hope so."

Father Burke left to complete his morning duties, allowing Patrick to sleep again. Pushing the radio's power on button, he looked content for the first time, in a long time. Without a final thought, he fell asleep mere moments before the radio DJ offered to give away a prize for the "Phrase That Pays."

§§§§

He again woke, feeling restful when Gregory silently breezed in, plopping down a lone breakfast tray. Patrick sat upright, moving the stand closer to his bed. He uncovered the grub, dissecting the sight of a large lump of kind of yellow scrambled eggs stuck to a plate. But Patrick was ravenous and feeling industrious. He energetically opened his top junk food drawer, groped, before pulling out empty candy wrappers and papers. Finally, he located a handful of ketchup packets and a bag of Cheez-Its.

Patrick bit open the small containers, squirting the runny, red tomato paste on the egg pile. He then added a generous amount of pepper, a dab of salt, mixing and mashing the remaining imitation cheese-flavored chips into the mush with a single fork. Finally, he scooped the finished cuisine onto a piece of brick-hard, cold toast. He took a brave taste, nibble, bite, swallowing before ultimately giving a luxuriated "not bad" smile at newly discovered culinary skills.

§§§§

As the passing hours ensued, Patrick recovered his energies, yearning to return home on his own accord. He sat alone on Pearl's stripped bed, his hands resting on the gray and black striped plastic-coated mattress.

He glanced at his own messy bed, as well as Tony's and Matt's, which were crisply made. Patrick's parents were expertly moving around the room packing his belongings, his mother placing the radio into the unusually, neatly organized duffel bag.

"I bet you can't wait to get back home, dear," she finally spoke.

His parents headed for the doorway, Dad carrying the duffle bag and guitar. Patrick jumped back into the ever-reliable wheelchair, but stopped at the room entrance as if stunned by an invisible force shield.

"What about the records?" his mother continued, pointing at the box sitting on the near windowsill.

"Oh, I'll leave them for the guys who will be taking over this room," he said. "Let me include a note, though. I'll meet you both at the elevator."

"Don't take too long," his father said, already worrying about city traffic. "I want us to hit the road so I can explain the new workout routine for this upcoming year. Think I finally figured how to make you strong enough for the braces."

"Dad," Patrick tried interrupting his father.

It was too late because Jack was on a roll. He dropped the bag and guitar without regard, whipping out a small spiral-bound notebook and pen from the blue blazer.

"Ok, perhaps it's too early to discuss my plan," he said resolutely, trying to control himself from sharing the ambitious regime. "You know, it probably can wait until tomorrow."

"Dad," Patrick tried again to unsuccessfully suppress his father's enthusiasm.

"Alright, I'll tell you now," Jack said, excitedly scribbling notes on a clean page. "We were focusing too much on bulk and strength. Now I've calculated what will make you mean and lean. I'm going to increase your endurance by starting you on a special protein diet and concentrate on short, multiple, light weightlifting repetitions."

"Dad," he repeated, grabbing the pad from his father's clutches. "Will you listen to me? I'm not walking again. You got it? Comprendo? We gave it our best shot, but it's not going to happen."

He placed the small, damaged notebook back in his dad's hands, wheeling in the direction of the room's sink. His father quickly followed.

"What do you mean it's not going to happen?" Jack Flannery said, taken aback.

"I'm going to spend the rest of my life using this wheelchair," Patrick attempted to explain.

"I, I don't understand," his dad said, now stuttering, his strategy faltering. "This is not my son Patrick speaking to me right now."

"You and I have to stop fighting about this," he implored, taking his father's hand.

Jack pulled away, walking back toward the door without either the guitar or duffle bag; he looked pleadingly at his wife who also appeared caught off guard by the sudden change in the conversation's tone.

"Dad, it's not your fault," he said, trying to relieve the tension. "It just didn't work out. I don't hate my wheelchair anymore. And I'm cool with how things worked out."

"We are dropping this subject," he barked, with conviction but clearly irritated. "Do you hear me? No son of mine is ever going to waste our past efforts."

"It's over," Patrick said, almost apologetically. "But I'm a lucky guy to have parents who pushed me hard. Dad, I'm going to be okay because of you and mom."

"I'll be waiting down the hallway," he whispered, looking nervously out the open door, probably fearful others might have heard their exchange.

"I love you, Dad," Patrick said, peacefully, not wanting to quarrel.

But Jack restrained from commenting, and instead, stormed by his wife who attempted to corral his arm. She glanced at the doorway and then back at Patrick who already picked up the duffle bag.

"I wish you would try to understand," she said leaning against his bed.

"It's okay, Mom," he said, mildly. "Really."

Mrs. Flannery began to quietly weep, confusing Patrick who vainly scoured for tissues after realizing the sink's wall-mounted paper towel dispenser was depleted. Eventually handing a clean, dry wash cloth he discovered on Matt's pristine bed with other freshly laid out linens. She wiped the streaming tears, dabbing her nostrils.

"Please don't cry," he spoke, holding her non-occupied hand.

"Patrick, I don't think you truly appreciate what your father endures every day of his life," she began, the devotion for her husband evident. "He loves you. I'm sorry if he made you believe he would love you more if you weren't using the wheelchair. Your father has a hard time not blaming himself for the accident. He, we shouldn't have let you play baseball that day."

"Mom."

His mother ignored him. "You didn't even want to play baseball, remember," she said to him. "You wanted to go swimming."

"You don't have to explain."

"But you had barely recovered from the chicken pox," she continued. "Your father and I wanted you to wait one more day before you went back into the pool. We thought we were making the right decision. What difference was a stupid day going to make?"

"You were both looking out for me," Patrick interrupted, defensively. "You made the decision out of love, Mom. You both need to let it go."

"I'm not sure he'll ever be able to do that," she said, reluctantly. "That's something you need to accept."

"It's no one's fault...," Patrick remarked. "...except for maybe the drunken guy getting behind the wheel of his car."

"Not a day goes by without me still wanting to strangle that, that bastard," Mrs. Flannery, blurted.

"Mom, did you just say bastard?" Patrick asked, thinking those were the harshest words ever to flow from her mouth.

"Please go easy on your father," Mrs. Flannery, again pleaded. "He does love you. He loves all of us. And I love him. Your dad always thought he needed to push you harder after the accident. For better or worse, whether it's right or wrong, that's who he is."

Without another word she stood, lifted the guitar, and departed to join her life-long companion. Patrick could not help but notice the eerie silence in the room. For a moment, the soon-to-be-discharged patient was unsure what to do next. Remembering about the note, he headed toward the windowsill, writing a simple message on the box with the cheap, clear plastic blue Bic pen someone had mistakenly left behind. Hesitating, he viewed the room and its empty beds. Using his teeth, Patrick superstitiously tore the blue hospital name-tag off his wrist, wheeled to his bed and expertly tied it, like he had the others, to the frame.

A knock on the open door startled him, causing him to jump and bang his head against the nightstand. While rubbing the sore scalp, he looked up to find Dr. Goodman standing next to him.

"Doctor."

"Sorry, I did not mean to scare you," he said mildly, pulling up a chair. "How are you feeling today?"

"I'm fine," Patrick said, with little emotion. "What about Pearl, though? He didn't have anyone."

"The hospital is taking care of his funeral."

Watching the always reassuring medical man, Patrick found himself saddened when thinking of his deceased roommate. Frankly, he knew little about him, causing Patrick to feel selfish for not pushing Pearl to provide more personal information. Who was this gifted artist? Where did he inherit the many possessed talents?

"In a strange way, I'm going to miss this room," he said plaintively, lamenting his departure. "Every time I'm admitted it becomes my personal sanctum."

"I understand," said Dr. Goodman. "It's been an interesting week for you."

Patrick opened his eyes but did not reply, sensing the doctor had heard similar comments from past patients. As much as he wanted to leave and be back in the family home, he strangely found himself anxious when checking out of this annual cocoon.

"Edie Miller just told me about your decision," Dr. Goodman said. "Are you sure? There's talk about radical lighter braces being patented next year. We should keep our options open, but it's your prerogative"

"I love you, Doc," Patrick said, answering without a preamble.

The good doctor gradually raised his aging body from the taxing hard chair. Before he completely separated himself from it, Patrick leaned in for the annual good-bye cheek peck. However, the older man politely waved him off, and instead extended a hand, the one with the missing fingers, for him to shake.

"You're no longer one of my young patients."

He observed the doctor respond to a page as he disappeared, considering for the last time the box of records on the windowsill, then the four empty beds, before purposely leaving the room door open.

§§§§

Patrick joined his parents at the bank of elevators, when he saw one out-of-service. The dark pit was barricaded by a flimsy rope attached to unsecured orange rubber cones. He could not mistake the elevator as the very one that trapped Pearl and him only hours before. An irritated maintenance worker, laid flat on the floor, shouting down the shaft to mysterious comrades, in between bites of an oversized glazed donut.

Jack stepped away when his son wheeled up. However, Patrick still slow-motioned a punch to his solid flat stomach. Acting oblivious to the sign of affection, he instead considered Sister Margaret as she joined them.

"Sneaking out on us again, are you?" she said, sensing tenseness between father and son.

"Uh, no," Jack said honestly, smiling at his favorite nun. "See you next year."

She tussled Patrick's thick mop with both hands, regarding him with a telling look after pulling back. "Next year you will be too old for my floor," she informed him. "You will be staying upstairs in the adult ward. But I expect daily visits."

A young child began screaming at the opposite end of the hallway, the volume increasing as the wailing toddler, Tito, drew nearer. He clutched the black and white panda bear, running toward Jack, holding onto his legs for dear life after reaching him. A breathless Priscilla, her hair askew, pursued a few feet behind.

A moment ago, Tito was in his room showing off the stuffed animal to an already envious older child in the next crib when he detected the Flannery members pass, one-by-one. But when Patrick wheeled by dressed in the street attire he wore when arriving, the child correctly assumed something was surely amiss. Could Patrick be departing for good? If so, Tito was shocked since he had not discerned that information in any recent, overheard conversations.

Si, his parents were from Puerto Rico, and Spanish was his first language, but Tito felt no need to tell anyone, including the hospital staff, he comprehended English much better than imagined. Already the guarded child knew there was little reason to tell people, even those who pretended to love him, everything.

But he greatly feared being returned to his parents. Tito knew short-term it was inevitable, but he also sensed dire consequences, even greater bodily harm, specifically to his body, might occur if and when that happened. The boy constantly dreamed of a day when someone, some couple, some family would stumble upon him, only to fall in love with his contagious benign disposition. Secretly, he sensed a bond and attraction when he met the Flannery family, especially Jack, in the lobby earlier this week. The stuffed animal gift surely was an initial step before he would become Patrick's new little brother, he had immaturely concluded. But they were leaving, and most likely forever. Their exodus was surely his eventual death sentence, he feared.

"Tito, espera," Priscilla inhaled, trying to catch her breath.

She attempted to pry the near hysterical boy off Jack's legs. "No, no, no, no go," he cried, choking between words. "No te vayas. Quedate. You stay."

Jack, although surprised, lifted the quivering little boy into his arms. "Tito, Tito," he said softly with great affection. "We have to take my son home."

"No te vayas," he continued crying, alternating between Spanish and English. "Quedate. No go."

Priscilla gently took Tito from Jack, holding him close to her chest. The nurse continued comforting the obedient, but upset, boy until he finally calmed down. Defeated, he simply rested his head against her breasts, teary eyes wide-open.

"Come, Tito. Let's get you some ice cream," she suggested. "Vamos a comprar un helado."

They walked away, with Tito embracing the panda. An operable elevator arrived, surprisingly stopping flush with the hospital floor. "As you can see, the hospital finally hired a new elevator contractor," Sister

Margaret said gleefully, pointing at the moody worker who was working on a second glazed donut.

Patrick and his parents entered the elevator, but his father turned to speak with the nun before any cab button was pushed. "Where will the little boy go after his wounds heal?" Jack inquired.

"Even after these unspeakable, unnatural hardships, the courts have still granted Tito's parents custody," Sister Margaret sighed. "They get him back on Tuesday. We can only pray he'll be safe. Good-bye, Flannery family. Good-bye, Patrick."

Their door closed as another opened. A frightened teenager, using an electric wheelchair, buzzed out, his parents followed, lugging several mismatched luggage pieces. The pink lady, scurried out, carrying the required medical chart.

"Here is Hugh, one of your new check-ins," she said, hesitantly, handing the chart to the no-nonsense nun before racing back into the waiting lift. "Two others are downstairs being processed for admittance."

"Welcome," she said to the strangers, her voice animated.

Sister Margaret, Hugh, and his parents headed down the long corridor toward Patrick's former room.

§§§§

Patrick parked his wheelchair on the sidewalk, letting the end-of-summer blazing sun bake an already pinkish face, as he patiently waited for his parents. Preoccupied hospital personnel, as well as other New

York City residents, busily walked around him, heading to their lunchtime destinations.

Suddenly the roar of an approaching motorcycle caught his attention, forcing Patrick to turn in the direction of the vulgar noise. Yet an even louder racket could be heard over the din. It was moments before Patrick realized it was Tony's voice, shouting his name, while steering the frequently mentioned Harley toward where he sat.

"Yo, roomie," he shouted. "Wait up."

Although typically a reckless driver, Tony meticulously parked his Harley just a few feet away before removing his helmet and dismounting the black painted bike.

"Check it out, Ironside," he said, still unnecessarily screaming. "Now dese are wheels, ya know."

Patrick did not offer a reply.

"Hey, about da other night," Tony continued surprisingly genially.

"Don't worry about it," Patrick said loathingly, cutting Tony off, his temper festering. "Listen, I have to hit the road."

"I wanted to, ya know, get here before you and Pearl left," Tony said. "Is he still inside?"

"Yeah, he is," Patrick responded, sarcastically, with a piercing look.

"Good," Tony said. "I'll go see 'em."

"No you won't," he said, deadpanned, opening up. "Pearl's dead."

"What the fuck?"

"He overdosed on heroin after you and I spoke on the phone," he continued in a rising fury.

"Jesus...Well, ya know, once a druggie, always a druggie," he said, callously laughing without pausing.

"What did you say?" he asked, shocked at the lack of fidelity, Patrick tightly gripped his wheels.

"A druggie? I can't believe you said that. He's your friend. Pearl was your friend."

Strangely, Tony found the remark humorous, letting out a loud hoot. "My friend?" he asked when finishing the laugh. "Hey, man, my boys, they're my friends. Ya know, my boys at home was right, ya can never really know a nigga."

Had it been another day, another time, he would continue the fight, but Patrick was summarily tired and simply wanted to leave the city. "I have to go," he said sneeringly.

He pivoted to depart, catching Tony off guard, who looked defensively around at the passing pedestrians. "Where's ya goin'?" he called out, confused, as the wheelchair rolled away.

"Come on, what did I say? Where ya goin'" Tony asked again, louder. "Ya didn't even check out my bike."

Patrick looked at the verdant roommate one final time, feeling a sudden pang. "Take care of yourself, Tony," he said mildly, pushing himself down the block.

A somewhat embarrassed Tony absorbed his remark without comment. He stared at the departing Patrick, as the Flannery family station wagon pulled up to the nearby corner. But he simply shrugged, put on his customized painted helmet, mounted the Harley, only to drive away in the opposite direction, back to his waiting Brooklyn cocoon.

§§§§

Jack collapsed the wheelchair and in one swinging motion, threw it into the rear wagon compartment. He slammed shut the panel door, walking toward the driver's seat while wiping his wet forehead with a fresh, Escher-patterned linen handkerchief. No longer angry with his son, he waited, hoping Patrick would speak first. Mrs. Flannery sat in the front passenger seat intently working the day's *New York Times* crossword puzzle. She could sense whatever stress existed between her two men had evaporated, allowing them to enjoy the scenic trip home.

Patrick, oblivious to their endeavors, leaned his head out the open car window to escape the oppressive non-air conditioned conditions.

Looking out, he was stunned to notice Edie standing alone at the street corner next to a popular food vendor wagon wearing cranberry PT garb. The dark-skinned Pakistani cart owner handed her a canned cold drink and dripping hot dog, both wrapped in soggy napkins.

Jack folded the handkerchief, trying to follow the ironed creases, but then impatiently stuffed it into his back pants pocket, before entering the car. He turned the key in the ignition, simultaneously starting both the engine and conversation with his wife. He eased the family vehicle into the closest traffic lane, heading toward the corner where Edie stoically stood with her purchased transient meal, as exhaust fumes undulated over the city street pavement.

An opportune timed red light forced their auto to stop next to her and the food vendor. Patrick kept his gaze, watching with amusement as she bit into the snappish, messy frank, oozing yellow mustard on her lower lip. A warm wind blew wisps of hair across Edie's face interfering with her ability to conquer the waiting dog and bun.

Patrick observed, looking through the still-opened car window, as Edie, attempting to wipe away the bright condiment with her tongue, spied him. After an awkward moment, they smiled in concert, first tentatively, then happily. The light turned green allowing his father to press heavily on the gas pedal, proceeding through the intersection.

They regarded each other in wonderment, their smiles intact. Patrick continued looking back to watch Edie until she became lost in the sea of city traffic and people.

About The Author

Kevin Gerard McGuire grew up in a large Irish-Catholic family in Newburgh, New York. At the age of seven, he was struck by an intoxicated driver while playing baseball, and has used a wheelchair ever since. Although many see his story as a tragedy, Kevin has been able to overcome many obstacles and lead a rich, fulfilling life.

His professional career has been dedicated to improving the quality of life for people with disabilities. A graduate of Georgetown University Law School and the founder of McGuire Associates (mcguireassociatesinc.com), he advises professional sports teams, the owners of large-capacity concert venues, and some of the country's leading architects about effectively and proactively meeting the standards of the Americans with Disabilities Act.

In addition to his consulting firm, Kevin has also created AbleRoad (ableroad.com), a website and smartphone application that connects people with accessible places.

For more information about PATRICK, visit the official book website at patricknovel.com.

Made in the USA
Charleston, SC
23 August 2013